"Did you k[now] the infor[mation] without y[our] [h]aving to seduce me?" Elizabeth asked.

Joe sighed. "Doc, this situation isn't the same. You came into this knowing the mission."

Elizabeth's gaze narrowed ever so slightly. "Did I really?"

He had to smile. "To the extent you needed to know, yes."

"But you didn't answer my question," she countered, refusing to give an inch. "Would you have resorted to seducing me if necessary?"

"I had my orders, Doc, and seducing you wasn't included." When she would have turned to leave, he caught her wrist once more and drew her back. "Had I not been restrained by my orders, I can't say I wouldn't have tried. But the effort wouldn't have been about the mission."

DEBRA WEBB

PERSON OF INTEREST

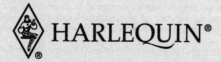

HARLEQUIN®

TORONTO • NEW YORK • LONDON
AMSTERDAM • PARIS • SYDNEY • HAMBURG
STOCKHOLM • ATHENS • TOKYO • MILAN • MADRID
PRAGUE • WARSAW • BUDAPEST • AUCKLAND

There are people in our lives we encounter who make their marks. Those
who leave some indelible influence on who and what we will become.
But if we're really lucky, there are those whose presence in our lives
makes a difference that goes so much deeper than the skin that our life
would not have been what it was destined to be without them. This book
is dedicated to one such person with whom I have had the pleasure of
love and laughter and the overwhelming sorrow of loss and grief.
To my baby brother, John Brashier. You are my soul's twin.
Never forget how very much I love you.

ISBN 0-373-22891-0

PERSON OF INTEREST

Copyright © 2006 by Debra Webb

www.eHarlequin.com

Printed in U.S.A.

ABOUT THE AUTHOR

Debra Webb was born in Scottsboro, Alabama, to parents who taught her that anything is possible if you want it badly enough. She began writing at age nine. Eventually she met and married the man of her dreams, and tried some other occupations, including selling vacuum cleaners, working in a factory, a day-care center, a hospital and a department store. When her husband joined the military, they moved to Berlin, Germany, and Debra became a secretary in the commanding general's office. By 1985 they were back in the States, and finally moved to Tennessee, to a small town where everyone knows everyone else. With the support of her husband and two beautiful daughters, Debra took up writing again, looking to mystery and movies for inspiration. In 1998, her dream of writing for Harlequin came true. You can write to Debra with your comments at P.O. Box 64, Huntland, Tennessee 37345 or visit her Web site at www.debrawebb.com to find out exciting news about her next book.

Books by Debra Webb

CAST OF CHARACTERS

Joe Hennessey—One of the CIA's finest field operatives. He makes Elizabeth restless in her own skin but she recognizes him for what he is, another dangerous man.

Elizabeth Cameron—The best restorative cosmetic surgeon in the country. But has her secret work for the CIA merely created a target list?

Director Calder—Director of the CIA. Elizabeth is one of his greatest assets. He will do anything to protect her.

Director Allen—Director of field operations with the CIA. He has only one goal: stop whoever is behind the hits on his agents.

Agent Craig Dawson—Elizabeth's CIA handler. *Safe, quiet*, those are the two words that best describe Dawson. Elizabeth wonders why she can't be attracted to a man like him.

Agent David Maddox—The man who broke Elizabeth's heart even after his death. There are so many things she should have said to him...and obviously a few he should have said to her.

Agent Mike Stark—A competent agent who guards Elizabeth with his very life.

Dr. Jeffrey—One of Elizabeth's colleagues at her private clinic. Another example of just the right kind of guy she should be falling for. They have worked together for four years.

Chapter One

Finished.

With a satisfied sigh, Dr. Elizabeth Cameron surveyed the careful sutures and the prepatterned blocks of tissue she had harvested from inconspicuous donor sites. For this patient the best sites available had been her forearms and thighs which had miraculously escaped injury.

The tailored blocks of harvested tissue, comprised of skin, fat and blood vessels, were tediously inset into the face like pieces of a puzzle and circulation to the area immediately restored by delicate attachment to the facial artery.

Lastly, the newly defined tissue was sculpted to look, feel and behave like normal facial skin, with scars hidden in the facial planes. In a few weeks this patient would resume normal activities and no one outside her immediate family and friends would ever have to know that she had scarcely survived a fiery car crash that had literally melted a good portion of her youthful Miss Massachusetts face.

She would reach her twenty-first birthday next month with a face that looked identical to the one that had won her numerous accolades and trophies. More important, the young woman who had slipped into severe clinical depression and who had feared her life was over would now have a second chance.

"She's perfect, Doctor."

Elizabeth acknowledged her colleague's praise with a quick nod and stepped back from the operating table. With one final glance she took stock of the situation. The patient was stable. All was as it should be. "Finish up for me, Dr. Jeffrey," she told her senior surgical resident.

Pride welled in her chest as she watched a moment while her team completed the final preparations for transporting the patient to recovery. Yes, she had performed the surgery, but the whole team had been involved from day one beginning with the complete, computerized facial analysis. This victory had been achieved by the entire team, not just one person. A team Elizabeth had handpicked over the past three years.

In the scrub room she stripped off her bloody gloves, surgical gown and mask, then cleaned her eyeglasses. She'd tried adjusting to contacts, but just couldn't manage the transition. Sticking to the old reliables hadn't failed her yet. She was probably the only doctor in the hospital who still preferred to do a number of things the old-fashioned way. Like working with a certain team day in and day out. She'd worked with Jeffrey long enough now that they could anticipate each other's moves and needs ahead of time. It worked. She liked sticking with what worked.

Exhaustion clawed at her. The muscles of her shoulders quivered with fatigue, the good kind. This one had been a long, arduous journey for both patient and surgical team. Weeks ago the initial preparations had begun, including forming a mold from a sibling's right ear to use in building a replacement for the one the patient had lost in the accident. The size and symmetry had worked out beautifully.

No matter how painstakingly Elizabeth and her team prepared, she wasn't fully satisfied until she saw the completed work…until the patient was rolled to recovery. The time required to heal varied, three to six weeks generally with this sort of tissue transplanting. The swelling would lessen, the red lines would fade. And the new face would bloom like a rose in the sun's light, as close to nature's work as man could come.

As Elizabeth started for the exit, intent on going straight home and crashing for a couple of hours, the rest of the team poured into the scrub room, high-fives and cheers of elation rumbling through the group. Elizabeth smiled. She had herself a hell of a team here. They were the best, each topping his or her field of expertise, and they were good folks, lacking the usual "ego" that often haunted the specialized medical profession.

"Excellent work, boys and girls," she called to the highly trained professionals who were quickly regressing to more adolescent behavior as the adrenaline high peaked and then drained away. "See you in two weeks."

Elizabeth pushed through the doors and into the long, white sterile corridor, still smiling as the ruckus followed her into the strictly enforced quiet zone. She inhaled deeply of the medicinal smells, the familiar scents comforting, relaxing. This place was her real home. She spent far more time here than inside the four walls of the little brownstone on which she made a monthly mortgage payment. Not really a good thing, she had begun to see. She didn't like the slightly cynical, fiercely focused person she was turning into.

A change was definitely in order.

Two weeks.

She hadn't taken that much time off since—

She banished the memory before it latched on to her thoughts. No way was she going to dredge up that painful past. Two months had elapsed. She clenched her jaw and paused at the bank of elevators. Giving the call button a quick stab, she waited, her impatience mounting with each passing second. She loved her work, was fully devoted to it. But she desperately needed this time to get away, to put the past behind her once and for all. She had to move on. Regain her perspective…her balance.

The elevator doors slid open and Elizabeth produced a smile for the nurses who exited. Almost three o'clock in the afternoon, shift change. The nurses and residents on duty would brief those arriving for second shift on the status of their patients. Orders would be reviewed and the flow of patient care would continue without interruption.

Dr. Jeffrey would stay with her patient for a time and issue the final orders. There was nothing for Elizabeth to worry about. She boarded the elevator and relaxed against the far wall. Her eyes closed as she considered the cruise she'd booked just last week. A snap decision, something she never, ever did. Her secretary had insisted she could not spend her time off at home or loitering around her office. Which, in retrospect, Elizabeth had to admit was an excellent idea. Hanging around the house or office, organizing books and files or personal items that were already in perfect order, would not be in her best interest. The last thing she needed in her life was more order.

Making a quick stop at the second-floor staff lounge to pick up her sweater and purse, more good-byes were exchanged with coworkers who couldn't believe she was actually going to take a vacation. Elizabeth shook her head in self-deprecation. She really had lost any sense of balance. Work was all she had, it seemed, and everyone had taken notice. One way or another she intended to change that sad fact.

Hurrying through Georgetown University Medical Center's expansive lobby, she made her way to the exit that led to the employee parking garage. She could already see herself driving across the District, escaping everything. As much as she loved D.C., she needed to get away, to mingle with the opposite sex. To start something new and fresh. To put *him* out of her mind forever. He was gone. Dead. He'd died in some foreign country, location unspecified, of unnatural causes probably, the manner unspecified. His body had not been recovered, at least, as far as she knew. He was simply gone. He wouldn't be showing up at her door in the middle of the night with an unexpected forty-eight-hour furlough he wanted to spend only with her.

Stolen moments. That was all she and Special Agent David Maddox had really ever shared. But then, that was what happened when one fell in love with a CIA agent. Covert operations, classified missions, need-to-know. All familiar terms.

Too familiar, she realized as she hesitated mid-stride on the lower level of the parking garage, her gaze landing on her white Lexus—or more specifically on the two well-dressed men waiting next to the classy automobile.

One man she recognized instantly as Craig Dawson, her CIA handler. All valuable CIA assets had handlers. It was some sort of rule. He'd replaced David when their relationship had gotten personal. There were times when Elizabeth wondered if that change in the dynamics of the interaction between them had ultimately caused David's death. His work had seemed so much safer when he'd been her handler.

Stop it, she ordered. Thinking about the past was destructive. She knew it. The counselor the Agency had insisted she see after David's death had said the same. Face forward, focus on the future.

Her new motto.

Time to move on.

If only her past would stop interfering.

What did Agent Dawson want today of all days? Annoyance lined her brow. Whenever he showed up like this it could only mean a ripple in her agenda. She couldn't change her current plans. It had taken too long for her to work up the courage and enthusiasm to make them.

Her irritation mounting unreasonably, her attention shifted slightly. To the man standing next to Dawson. Another secret agent, no doubt. The guy could have been a carbon copy of Dawson from the neck down, great suit, navy in color, spit and polished black leather shoes. The only characteristics that differentiated the two were age and hair color.

Well, okay, that was an exaggeration, the two looked nothing alike. Dawson was fifty or so, distinguished-looking, with a sparkling personality. He'd never performed field duty for the CIA, was more the "office" type. The other guy looked younger, late-thirties maybe, handsome in a rugged sort of way, and his expression resembled that of a slick gangster. At least what she could see of it with him wearing those dark shades. The five o'clock shadow on his lean jaw didn't help. Her gaze lingered there a moment longer. Something about his profile…his mouth seemed familiar.

She rarely forgot a face, and this one made her nervous. She looked away, settling her gaze back on Dawson and the kind of familiarity she could trust. Maybe she had run into the other man before. But that didn't seem likely since her dealings with the CIA had always come through David or Agent Dawson, discounting her rare command performance with the director himself. A frown nagged at her brow. It was doubtful that she knew the other man, yet something about him seriously intimidated her. Not a good thing in a CIA agent, to her way of thinking.

But then, what did she know? She was only a part-time volunteer agent whose existence was strictly off any official records. And she hadn't even been subjected to the training program. Calling herself an agent was a stretch. She actually had no dealings whatsoever with the CIA other than performing the occasional professional service for which she refused to accept pay. To date, she had provided new faces for more than a dozen deep-cover operatives. It was the least she could do for her country—why would she allow payment for services rendered? Elizabeth saw it as her patriotic duty. The covert sideline was her one secret…her one departure from the dull routine of being Dr. Elizabeth Cameron.

"Dr. Cameron," Dawson said when she made no move to come closer, "the director would like to see you."

Elizabeth hiked her purse strap a little farther up her shoulder and crossed her arms over her chest. "I'm going on vacation, Agent Dawson," she said firmly as she ordered her feet to move toward her car. It was her car, after all, he couldn't keep her from getting in it and driving away. At least she didn't think he could.

"The meeting will only take a few minutes, ma'am," Dawson assured quietly while his cohort stood by, ominously silent, doing the *intimidation* thing.

She considered asking Craig if he was training a new recruit or if he'd worried that he might need backup for bringing her in. But she doubted he'd get the joke. She wouldn't have gotten it either until about a week ago. That's when she'd made her decision. The decision to put some spontaneity into her life. She was sick of being plain old quiet, reserved Elizabeth who never varied her routine. Who stuck with what worked and avoided personal risk at all cost. She got out of bed at the same time every morning, showered, readied for work and ate a vitamin-enhanced meal bar on the way to the office. After ten or twelve hours at the office and/or hospital, she worked out at the fitness center and went home, took a relaxing hot bath and fell into bed utterly exhausted.

Same thing, day in and day out.

She couldn't even remember the last time she'd gone to a movie much less had a simple dinner date.

But no more.

Still, she had an obligation to the CIA. She'd promised to help out when they needed her. Right now might be inconvenient but it was her duty to at least listen to what they needed. Growing up a military brat had taught her two things if nothing else:

always guard your feelings and never, ever forget those who risk their lives for your freedom. Guarding her feelings was a hard-learned skill, the knowledge gained from moving every two to three years and having to fit in someplace new. The other—well, patriotism was simply something every good American should practice.

"All right," she relented to Mr. Dawson's obvious relief. "I'll see him, for a few minutes only." She held up a hand when Dawson would have moved toward the dark sedan parked next to her car. "Anything else he needs will have to wait until I get back from my cruise," she said just to be sure he fully grasped the situation. "Even doctors take vacations."

"I understand, ma'am," Dawson confirmed with a pleasant smile. But something about the smirk on the other man's face gave her pause. Did he know her? She just couldn't shake that vague sense of recognition. Maybe he was privy to what the director wanted and already knew she was in for a battle if she wanted this vacation to happen.

She was still a private citizen. She accepted no money for her work and she had never refused the Agency's requests. But this time she just might.

Elizabeth settled into the back seat of the dark sedan and Dawson closed her door before sliding behind the steering wheel. The other man took the front passenger seat, snapped the safety belt into place and stared straight ahead. Elizabeth was glad he hadn't opted to sit in back with her. She didn't like the guy. He made her feel threatened on some level. A frown inched its way across her forehead. She had to admit that he was the first Agency staff member she'd met who actually looked like one of the guys depicted in the movies. Thick, dark hair slicked back. Concealing eyewear, flinty profile. She shivered, then pushed the silly notion away.

She wanted spontaneity in her life, not trouble. This guy had trouble written all over what she could see of that too handsome face. Upon further consideration, she decided it was his mouth that disturbed her the most. There was a kind of insolence about it…a smugness that shouted *I could kiss you right now and make you like it.*

Another shudder quaked through her and she reminded herself of what falling for a spy had cost her already.

CIA agents did not make for reliable companions. She knew better than most. A pang of old hurt knifed through her. She'd made a mistake, veered too close to the flame and she'd gotten burned.

Never again.

If she fell in love a second time, which was highly doubtful considering her current track record, it would be with someone safe, someone predictable.

Safe.

At one time she'd considered David safe.

But she'd been wrong.

He'd felt safe and comfortable, but it had been nothing but an illusion.

David Maddox had been every bit as dangerous— as much of an adrenaline junkie—as all the rest in his line of work. CIA agents were like cops; they thrived in high-tension situations, on the thrill of the hunt. No matter how quiet and reserved David had pretended to be, he'd been just like the rest of them.

Just like Craig Dawson and his companion.

Men willing to risk it all for their country, who broke hearts and left shattered lives.

She didn't want that kind of man.

Never again.

Elizabeth focused on the passing landscape, refused to dwell on the subject. The skyscrapers and bumper-to-bumper traffic of the D.C. area eventually gave way to trees and only the occasional passing motorist. It seemed odd to Elizabeth that the CIA's headquarters would be nestled away in the woods, seemingly in the middle of nowhere, like a harmless, sprawling farm. But there was nothing harmless about the vast property. Security fences topped with concertina wire and cameras. Warnings about entering the premises with electronic devices. Armed guards. Definitely not harmless in any sense of the word.

Dawson braked to a stop and flashed his ID for the guard waiting at the entrance gate while another guard circled the sedan with a dog trained to sniff out explosives and the like. Even now she imagined that high-tech gadgets were monitoring any conversation that might take place inside the vehicle. Every word, every nuance in tone scrutinized for possible threat.

The recruits here were trained to infiltrate, interrogate, analyze data and to kill if necessary. Their existence and proper training were essential to national security, she understood that. Respected those who sacrificed so very much. But she couldn't bring herself to feel comfortable here. It took a special kind of human being to fit into this world. Her gaze flitted to the man in the front passenger seat. A man like him. Dark, quiet, enigmatic. A man fully prepared to die…to kill…for what he believed in.

A dangerous man.

But not dangerous to her…never again. No more dangerous men in her life, she promised herself as she did her level best to ignore the premonition of dread welling in her chest. Safe. Occasionally spontaneous maybe, but safe. She had her new life all mapped out and the dead last thing it included was danger.

Chapter Two

The main lobby of the CIA headquarters always took Elizabeth's breath away. The granite wall with its stars honoring fallen agents. The flags and statues… the grandeur that represented the solemn undertaking of all those who risked their lives to make the world a safer place. The shadow warriors.

Elizabeth looked away from that honorary wall, knowing that one of those stars represented David. Though she would never know which one since his name would not be listed. *Anonymous even in death.*

For the first time since his death she wondered if she'd known him at all. Was his name even David Maddox?

Her heart squeezed instantly at the thought. This was precisely why she had promised herself she would not think about the past. Not today, not any day.

She had to get on with the present, move into the future.

Like David, the past was over. She was thirty-seven for Christ's sake. Her fantasy of some day having a family was swiftly slipping away. Never before had she been so keenly aware of just how much time she had wasted. Though she loved her work, she didn't regret for a moment the sacrifices she had made to become the respected surgeon she was; it was time to have a personal life as well.

The rubber soles of her running shoes whispered against the gleaming granite floor where the CIA's emblem sprawled proudly, welcoming all who entered. The guards and the metal detectors beyond that proved a little less welcoming, reminding Elizabeth of the threat that loomed wherever government offices could be found. Even in her lifetime the world had changed so much. Maybe part of her sudden impatience to move forward was somehow related to current events as well as the recent past. Whatever the case, it was the right thing to do.

Dawson led her to the bank of elevators and depressed the down button. Uneasiness stirred inside her again. Somehow she doubted that the director's office had been moved to the basement. Before she could question his selection the doors slid open and the three of them boarded the waiting car.

When he selected a lower level, she felt compelled to ask, "Aren't we going to the director's office?"

Agent Dawson smiled kindly. He'd always had a nice smile, a calming demeanor. She was glad for that. "We're meeting in a special conference room this time. The director is there now waiting for your arrival."

Elizabeth managed a curt nod, still feeling a bit uneasy with the situation despite her handler's assurances. The fine hairs on the back of her neck stood on end the way they did whenever she sensed a deviation in the status quo of a patient's condition. She could always predict when things were about to go wrong. This felt wrong. For the first time since she'd agreed to support the CIA from time to time, she felt seriously uncomfortable with the arrangement. That premonition of dread just wouldn't go away though it refused to clarify itself fully.

The other agent, the one whose presence added to her discomfort and who hadn't been introduced to her as of yet, shifted slightly, drawing her attention in his direction.

He still wore those confounding sunglasses. Elizabeth found the continued behavior to be rude and purposely intimidating. Fury fueling an uncharacteristic boldness she opened her mouth to say just that and he looked at her. Turned his head toward her, tilting it slightly downward and looked straight at her as if he'd sensed her intent. She didn't have to see his eyes. She could feel him watching her. Something fierce surged through her. Fear, she told herself. But it didn't feel quite like fear.

Who the hell was this man?

She swung her attention back to Agent Dawson, intent on demanding the identity of the other man, but the elevator bumped to a halt. The doors yawned open and Dawson motioned for her to precede him. Pushing her irrational annoyance with the other man to the back burner, she stepped out of the car and moved in the direction Dawson indicated. She would likely never see this stranger again after today, what was the point in making a scene?

ON SOME LEVEL she recognized him. Special Agent Joe Hennessey couldn't jeopardize this mission by allowing her to recognize him before the decision was made. He'd kept the concealing eyewear in place to throw her off, but he had a feeling she wouldn't be fooled for long. He'd been careful not to speak and not to get too close.

But there was no denying the chemistry that still sizzled between them…it was there in full force. He could only hope that she was disconcerted with the unexpected trip to Langley and was off balance enough to give a commitment before the full ramifications of the situation became crystal clear.

The long corridor stretched out before them, the occasional door on one side or the other interrupting the monotonous white walls. Tile polished to a high sheen flowed like an endless sea of glass. Surface mounted fluorescent lights provided ample lighting if not an elegant atmosphere. He could feel her uneasiness growing with each step. She didn't like this deviation from the usual routine.

Hennessey knew this was her first trip to the bowels of the Agency and she probably hoped it would be the last. The adrenaline no doubt pumping through her veins would make the air feel heavier, thicker. It didn't take a psychic to know she was seriously antsy in the situation. Didn't like it one damned bit.

Dawson stayed to her right, a step ahead, leading the way. Hennessey stayed to her left, kept his movements perfectly aligned with hers, not moving ahead, never falling behind. If the overhead lights were to suddenly go out and the generators were to fail, he would still know she was there. He could *feel* her next to him. For someone who loved clinging to a routine, her energy was strong…her presence nearly overwhelming. With every fiber of his being he knew she was even now scrolling through her memory banks searching for what it was that felt familiar about him.

Thankfully they reached their destination. Dawson stopped at the next door on the left. "The director is waiting for you inside, Dr. Cameron." He reached for the door and opened it.

Elizabeth looked from him to Hennessey and back. "Aren't you coming in, Agent Dawson?"

She didn't like this at all. Hennessey could feel the tension vibrating inside her mounting.

"Not this time, ma'am."

SHE DIDN'T LIKE THIS. Her frown deepening, Elizabeth pushed her glasses up the bridge of her nose and moved through the open door. She had been briefed long ago about the various levels of security clearances within the CIA. Some were so secret that even the designation was classified. In most cases, the rule that every agent lived by was the "need-to-know" rule. One knew what one needed to know and nothing more.

Clearly Agent Dawson and his friend didn't need to know whatever the director was about to discuss with her. The door closed behind her with a resolute thud and she shivered. The sound echoed through her, shaking loose a memory from months ago. It had been dark…she'd scarcely seen his face, but she had known his reputation. The man who'd been sent to protect her that night had held her there like a prisoner in the darkness for hours insisting that it was for her own safety. He'd been rude and arrogant, had

overwhelmed her with his brute strength…his absolute maleness. And then he'd been gone.

He'd almost taken advantage of her—she'd almost
let him—and then he'd disappeared. Like a shadow in
the night…as if he'd never been there at all. She'd
known what he'd done. He'd reveled in pushing her buttons, in making her weak. But she'd resisted, just barely.
If she hadn't, he would have taken full advantage, even
knowing that she belonged to David. She wondered if
David had ever suspected that the friend he'd sent to
protect her from a threat the nature of which she hadn't
been authorized clearance for had almost succeeded in
seducing her with his devastating charm. Some friend.

But then that was Special Agent Joe Hennessey.
He might be a superspy of legendary proportions, but
she knew him for what he was: ruthless and with an
allegiance only to himself. The guy waiting with
Dawson in the corridor reminded her of Hennessey.

"Elizabeth, thank you for coming."

Elizabeth shoved the distracting thoughts away
as Director George Calder rounded the end of the
long conference table and made his way to her. A second gentleman she didn't recognize rose from his
chair but didn't move toward her.

Present and future, forget the past, she reminded
her too forgetful self. Like David, Joe Hennessey
was a part of her past that was gone forever. Face for-

ward. Focus on the here and now…on the future. Director Calder took her hand in his and shook it firmly.

"I hope you'll forgive my intrusion into your vacation schedule," he offered, his expression displaying sincere regret.

George Calder was a tall, broad-shouldered man, not unlike the two agents waiting outside the door. Nearly sixty, his hair had long ago silvered and lines drawn by the execution of enormous power marred his distinguished face. He'd presented himself as nothing less than gracious and sensitive each time he'd requested Elizabeth's presence. But there was more this time. Something else simmered behind those intelligent hazel eyes. The sixth sense that usually centered on her patients was humming now, urging her to act.

"Technically," Elizabeth said succinctly, ignoring her foolish urge for fight or flight, "my vacation doesn't start until tomorrow so you're still safe for now."

George laughed, but the sound was forced. "Let me introduce you to our director of operations." He turned to the other man in the room. This one was slightly shorter and thinner, but looked every bit as formidable as Director Calder.

"Kurt Allen, meet our talented Dr. Elizabeth Cameron."

His fashionable gray pinstripe suit setting him apart from the requisite navy or black, Allen rushed to shake her hand, his smile wide and seeming genuine. "It's an honor to finally meet you, Dr. Cameron. Your work is amazing. I can't tell you how many of my best men you've spared."

Elizabeth realized then that Director Allen was in charge of the field agents who most often needed her services.

"I'm glad I can help, Director Allen," she told him in all sincerity. It felt odd now that she'd never met him before. Need-to-know, she reminded herself.

There was an awkward moment of tense silence before Calder said, "Elizabeth, please have a seat and we'll talk."

The director ushered her to the chair next to the one he'd vacated when she'd entered the room. Allen seated himself directly across the table from her.

The air suddenly thickened with the uneasy feel of a setup. This was not going to be the typical briefing. There was no folder marked *classified* that held the case facts of the agent who needed a new face. There was nothing but the high sheen of the mahogany conference table and the steady stares of the two men who obviously did not look forward to the discussion to come.

To get her mind off the intensity radiating around her, Elizabeth took a moment to survey the room. Richly paneled walls similar to that of the director's office several floors overhead gave the room a feeling of warmth. Royal blue commercial-grade carpet covered the floor. The array of flags surrounding the CIA emblem on the rear wall and the numerous plaques that lined the other three lent an air of importance to the environment. This was a place where discussions of national significance took place. She should feel honored to be here. Whatever she could do for the CIA was the least she could do for her country, she reminded herself.

Elizabeth clasped her hands atop the conference table, squared her shoulders and produced a smile for Director Calder. "Why did you need to see me, Director?" Someone had to break the ice. Neither of the gentlemen appeared prepared to dive in. Another oddity. What could either of these men, who possessed the power to start wars, fear from her?

Calder glanced at Allen then manufactured a smile of his own. "Elizabeth, I think you understand how important the Operations Directorate is here at the CIA."

She nodded. Though she actually knew little about the Operations Directorate, she did comprehend that the field operatives who risked their lives in positions deep undercover and generally in foreign countries came from that division.

"The men and women who make up the ranks of our field operatives are the very tip of the spear this agency represents," he went on, verifying her assumption. "They are the forerunners. The ones who provide us with the data that averts disaster. They risk more than anyone else."

Again she nodded her understanding. The knot in her stomach twisted as she considered why he felt the need to tediously prepare her for whatever it was he really wanted to say. Every instinct warned that things were not as they should be.

"During the past two and a half years we've counted on you more than a dozen times to provide a means of escape for our operatives. Your skill at creating new faces has allowed these men and women to avoid the enemy's vengeance while maintaining their careers. Without your help, a number of those operatives would certainly have lost their lives."

"There are other surgeons in your field," Allen interjected with a show of his palms for emphasis. "But not one in this country is as skilled as you."

Elizabeth blushed. She hated that she did that but there was no stopping it. She'd never taken compliments well. Though she worked hard and recognized that she deserved some amount of praise, it was simply a physical reaction over which she had no control. Her professional life was the one place where she suffered no doubts in regards to her competence.

If only she could harness some of that confidence for her personal life.

"I appreciate your saying so, Director Allen," she offered, "but I can't take full credit. My ability with the scalpel is a gift from God." She meant those words with all that made her who she was. A God complex was something she'd never had to wrestle with as so many of her colleagues did. She made it a point to remind her residents of that all important fact as well. Confidence was a good thing, arrogance was not.

Director Calder braced his hands on the table in front of him and drew her attention back to him, "That's part of the attitude that we hope will allow you to see the need for what we're about to ask of you, Elizabeth."

She didn't doubt her ability to handle whatever he asked of her. In that vein, she dismissed the uneasiness and lifted her chin in defiance of her own lingering uncertainty. There was only one way to cut to the chase here—be direct. "What is it you need, Director Calder. I've never turned you down before. Is there some reason you feel this time will be different?"

Two and a half years ago the CIA had, after noting her work in the field of restorative facial surgery, approached her. They needed her and she had gladly accepted the challenge. She would not change that course now.

"We are aware of the relationship you maintained with Agent Maddox," Allen broached, answering before Calder could or maybe because he didn't want to bring up the sensitive subject. "I believe the two of you were…intimate for more than a year before his death."

The oxygen in Elizabeth's lungs evacuated without further ado. She swallowed hard, sucked in a necessary breath and told her heart to calm. "That's correct." To say she was surprised by the subject would be a vast understatement. But, within this realm, there was no room for deception or hedging. Those traits were best utilized in the field. And the fact of the matter was Elizabeth had never been very good at lying. She was an open book. Subterfuge and confrontation were two of her least favorite strategies.

Just another reason she had no life. Real life, emotionally speaking, was too difficult. If she kept to herself, she wasn't likely to run into any problems.

But you're about to change that attitude, a little voice reminded. She had made up her mind to dive back into a social life…to take a few risks.

If only she could remember that mantra.

Director Calder picked up the conversation again, "Three months before his death Agent Maddox was involved in a mission that garnered this Agency critical information. He was, fortunately, able to complete the mission with his cover intact."

Elizabeth imagined that maintaining the validity of a cover would be crucial for future use. She nodded her understanding, prompting him to carry on.

"Though the group he infiltrated at the time was effectively eliminated, two members have moved into another arena which has created great concern for this agency."

Outright apprehension reared its ugly head. "I'm not sure I know what you mean." She did fully comprehend that there were certain elements she would not be told due to their classification, but she had to know more than this. Tap dancing around the issue wasn't going to assuage her uneasiness.

"The two subjects involved have relocated their operation here. On our soil," Allen clarified. "They have an agenda that we are not at liberty to disclose, but they must be stopped at all costs."

Elizabeth divided a look between the two men. Both wore poker faces, giving away nothing except determination. She hated to say anything that would make her look utterly stupid but her conclusion was simple. "If you know they're here, why don't you just arrest them or…or eliminate them."

Made sense to her. But then she was only a doctor, not a spy or an assassin. She felt certain they had some

legitimate reason for taking a less direct route to accomplish their ultimate goal, though she couldn't
begin to fathom what the motivation could possibly be.

"I wish it were that simple," Calder told her
thoughtfully. "Stopping the men they've sent won't
be enough. We have to know how they're getting their
information to ensure the threat is eliminated completely. Otherwise the root cause of the situation will
simply continue generating additional obstacles."

Now she got it. "You need these two members of
the group David infiltrated to lead you to their
source," she suggested. She'd seen a crime drama or
two in her life.

"Exactly," Allen confirmed. "If we don't find the
source, they'll just keep sending out more assassins."

Assassins. That meant targets.

"How does this involve me?" Her heart rate
kicked into overdrive. She moistened her lips as the
silence stretched out another ten seconds. This could
not be good.

Director Calder turned more fully toward her, fix-
ing her with a solemn gaze that reflected nearly as
much desperation as it did determination. "In order
to infiltrate this group we need someone with whom
they'll feel comfortable. Someone familiar. We have
an agent prepared to take the risk and infiltrate the
group, but we need to make a few alterations."

Her head moved up and down in acknowledgement. She was on the same page now. "You want me to give him a different appearance? A new face?" That's what she usually did. No big deal. But why all the beating around the proverbial bush?

"Correct," Calder allowed. "But just any face won't work. We'll be requesting a specific look."

"Someone these assassins know, feel comfortable with," she echoed his earlier words.

"Precisely," Allen agreed enthusiastically. "This part is crucial to the success of the mission. If the targets think for even a second that our man isn't who he says he is they'll kill him without hesitation. There is no margin for error whatsoever, Dr. Cameron. That's why your help is critical."

She looked expectantly from Calder to Allen and back. "What is it you need, *exactly*?" she asked, focusing her attention on Allen since he loved to throw around those extreme adverbs. The requirements sounded simple enough.

"What we need," Allen told her bluntly, "is David Maddox."

Her breath trapped in her throat and shock claimed her expression. She didn't need a mirror, she felt her face pinch in horrified disbelief. Her fingers fisted to fight back the old hurt. "David is dead," she replied with just as much bluntness as he'd issued the requirement. What was this man thinking?

Calder reached across the table and put his hand on hers. Echoes of the anguish she'd felt two months ago reverberated through her. "I know this is difficult, Elizabeth. You must believe that we wouldn't ask if there was any other way."

He was serious.

"Oh my God." She drew away from his comforting touch. Shook her head to clear it. This was too much. "How can you ask me this?"

"Dr. Cameron, there is no other option," Allen said flatly, his tone far cooler than before but his eyes reflected the desperation she'd already seen in Calder's. "We need David Maddox, but as you pointed out, he is dead. So we need a stand-in. We need you to do what you do best and give our agent David Maddox's face."

Tears stung her eyes, emotion clogged her throat, but somehow she managed to say the only thing she could. "I can't do that."

Director Calder leveled a steady gaze on hers. "I'm afraid my colleague is right, there is no other option, Elizabeth."

Chapter Three

Joe Hennessey waited with Craig Dawson in the corridor outside the conference room. He didn't have to be in the room or even watch the proceedings to know that Elizabeth Cameron would not like the idea. Not that he could blame her if he looked at it from her position but there were things she didn't know…would never know.

"She'll be okay with this," Dawson said quietly as if reading his mind.

Hennessey shrugged one shoulder. "She's your asset, you should know." His indifference might seem cold, but he had serious doubts where this whole operation was concerned. What the hell? He had a reputation for being cold and ruthless.

Dawson cut him a look that left no room for further discussion. He had faith in the woman even if he didn't have any in Hennessey.

Though Hennessey hadn't known David Maddox particularly well, he had met the woman in his life once. And once had been enough. Elizabeth Cameron had cool down to a science. Maybe she was hot between the sheets, but in Hennessey's estimation, a woman that reserved and uptight usually thought too much. Good, hot sex was definitely no thinking matter. It either was or it wasn't.

In his line of work he'd learned to take his pleasure where he could and not to linger for too long. Dr. Elizabeth Cameron was not the type to go for a thorough roll in the hay and then walk away. She was one of those women with a commitment fetish. She didn't do casual sex. Probably didn't even understand the concept. From what Hennessey had seen, the woman was all work and no play. Completely focused.

If she agreed to do the job, that would be a good thing. He damn sure didn't want a lesser surgeon screwing up his face. Not that he considered himself the Hollywood handsome type but he got his share of second looks. Including one or two from the good doctor. Though he doubted she would admit it in this lifetime. Just like before, she wanted to pretend there was nothing between them. In reality, there wasn't, not really. Just that one night. The night he'd saved her life but she would never own up to it. She would only remember his manhandling and overbearing attitude. But something had sparked between them that night…in the dark.

The chemistry had been there. Strong enough to startle him almost as much as it had her. She'd hated it and her extreme reaction had only made bad matters worse. But then, he loved a challenge. He'd felt the electricity between them again today. But like before, she'd wanted to ignore it. What did all that attraction say about the relationship she'd had with Maddox? Maybe there was a little bit of the devil in all of us, he mused, even the straitlaced doc.

Well, she might prefer to ignore him, but if the director had his way, she might as well get used to having him around. They would be spending the next three weeks in close quarters. Not that it would be a hardship. He thought about those long, satiny legs hidden beneath that conservative peach-colored skirt. The lady had a great body. She worked out. He'd watched her. She kept a hell of a boring routine. Yet there was no denying that blond hair and those green eyes were attractive even if she did make it a point to camouflage those long, silky tresses in a bun and those lovely green eyes behind the ugliest black rimmed glasses.

Well, attractive or not, hot in bed or not, Elizabeth Cameron held the key to his future. He hoped by now she understood that. His survival in the upcoming mission depended upon his ability to fool the enemy.

The idea of sporting another man's face held no real appeal, but if it got the job done Hennessey could deal with it. He could even manage to put up with the doc's company for a couple of weeks and maintain the necessary level of restraint. What he wasn't at all sure he could handle was her constant analysis.

He recalled quite well the way she'd studied him that one time. Her lover had apparently related a number of tales about the legendary Joe Hennessey, none of which had sat well with Miss Prim and Proper.

Half the stories were exaggerated and the other half were nobody's business. But that wouldn't keep her from holding his past, real or imagined, against him.

Hennessey put his life on the line for his country all the time. The last thing he deserved was some holier-than-thou broad, however talented, treating him like he was the scum of the earth. Throw that in the mix with the undeniable physical attraction and he came up with distraction.

He'd learned the hard way that if a guy thought with his privates in this business he ended up dead. He'd had his share of ladies along the way, but he never let one distract him from the mission.

He didn't intend to start now.

The door swung open and Hennessey came to attention. A leftover habit from his days in Special Forces. Anytime a superior officer was about, he came to attention as was expected.

Directors Calder and Allen moved into the corridor, closing the door behind them. A frown pulled at Hennessey's mouth. Where was the woman? He'd thought the plan was for him to be called in once they'd broken the news to her. Had she outright refused to do the job?

That would be just his luck. Damn. He wanted the best. And she was it.

"Agent Hennessey," Calder announced without preamble, "Dr. Cameron would like to see you now."

Hennessey blinked. "Alone?" He didn't relish the idea of the confrontation with no one else around to temper it.

Calder nodded. "She hasn't committed to the request. She insists on speaking to the operative assigned to the mission first. If she continues to resist, you have my authorization to enlighten her." He qualified his statement with a warning, "Her participation is essential, but she doesn't need to know any more than absolutely necessary."

With a heavy exhale and a nod of understanding, Hennessey stated for the record, "Yes, sir."

As he reached for the door, Dawson stopped him with a hand on his arm. "I know your reputation, Agent Hennessey," he cautioned quietly, "don't do anything you'll regret. Dr. Cameron is a nice lady."

"I think Agent Hennessey is aware of proper protocol," Director Calder suggested, his tone as stern as his expression. He would tolerate no roadblocks now or later. The reprimand was meant for both Dawson and Hennessey.

For the first time since going to the hospital to pick up the good doctor, Hennessey removed his eyewear. He'd worn the dark glasses inside purposely, to remain anonymous until the decision was final. Apparently there was going to be no help for that now. He hoped like hell she wouldn't let that one night influence her decision.

Hennessey leveled an unflinching stare on Dawson. "I have never jeopardized a mission or an asset."

"Just remember," Dawson persisted despite the director's warning, "that she is a very valuable asset."

Hennessey shoved his sunglasses back into place and opened the door. He didn't need Dawson telling him how to do his job. He had no intention of getting tangled up with Dr. Cameron. There might be some sexual energy bouncing back and forth between them, but she definitely was not his type.

Opinionated women were nothing but a pain in the ass.

Like he'd said before, some things don't require thought.

ELIZABETH COULDN'T SHAKE the idea that she knew the other agent. There was definitely something familiar about him. That mouth…the way his presence overwhelmed the atmosphere around him.

It couldn't be *him.*

She would remember if it was him. It wasn't like she could forget that night. That one night. She shivered. She'd tried not to think about it, but every now and then it poked through the layers of anger and guilt she'd piled on top of the memory. He'd practically held her hostage. He'd made her feel things she hadn't wanted to feel. A hot, searing ache, a yearning deep down inside her. It had been wrong. A betrayal. And with *him* no less. David had told her all about Special Agent Joe Hennessey. His dark, alluring charm that the ladies couldn't resist; his ruthless single-mindedness. An agent like no other.

She wondered if David would have spoken so highly of him if he'd known how close his supposed friend had come to seducing her…how close she'd come to allowing it?

Heat infused her cheeks, rushed over her skin at even the memory of those few hours. He'd cast a spell on her. Made her want to forget everything and everyone else. Thank God she'd come to her senses.

Chafing her arms she banished the disturbing memories. She had to figure this out…had to find a way to make them see that she could not do this. She simply couldn't do that to David's memory.

Only, David would want her to help.

If lives were in danger he would want her to do whatever necessary to help his fellow agents. But she needed more information. Surely they couldn't expect her to do this without further clarification.

And, dear God, could she do it?

Could she recreate David's face on another man?

SHE STOOD on the far side of the room, her back to the door. For about three seconds Hennessey hesitated, admiring the view. She might be a pain in the ass, but he could look at hers all day. Nice. All those hours on the stair-stepper clearly made a difference.

He closed the door, allowing it to slam just enough to get her attention. Startled, she whirled to face him.

The frown of utter confusion telegraphed her first thought loud and clear: *What the hell do you want?* She had no doubt expected the directors to return with their man in tow. The last person she'd expected to enter the room was him.

"Dr. Cameron, I'm Special Agent Joe Hennessey." As he moved toward her he reached upward and removed his concealing eyewear. "If you'll recall we met once before."

Her eyes rounded and that cute little mouth dropped open. "You!" The single word was cast like an accusing stone.

He tossed the glasses onto the conference table and propped a hip there. "You remember me," he offered, his smile infused with all the charm in his vast ladies' man repertoire.

She pointed to the door then to him, her confusion morphing into disbelief. "It's you he wants me to prepare for this mission?"

Hennessey flared his hands. "That's right. Is there a problem?"

Her head moved from side to side as all that confusion and disbelief coalesced into outrage. "You're nothing like David," she accused.

Well, she had that right but he saw no point in bursting her bubble where her former lover was concerned. "I'm the same height and build. The hair color is close enough, the eyes will be an easy fix with colored contacts." He shrugged, the control necessary to hold back his own patience slipping just a little. "I don't see the problem."

She blinked rapidly, her head doing that side-to-side thing again as if the very idea was blasphemy. "You're not *like* David," she argued.

He pushed off the table and moved toward her, lowering his voice an octave, slowing the cadence of his words as he recalled the numerous taped conversations he'd listened to. "I can do anything it takes to get the job done, *Elizabeth.*" Her head snapped up at his use of her first name. He said it with emphasis, the same way Maddox used to. "You'd be surprised at just how versatile I am."

Her pupils flared. She shivered. But it was the little hitch in her breathing that actually got to him, made his pulse skitter and chinked the armor he wore to protect his emotions. He shook his head and looked away. How the hell had he let that happen?

"You expect me to trust anything you say?"

Well, she had him pegged, didn't she? Apparently she'd accepted every rumor she'd heard as fact. "Bottom line, Doc, I can't do this without you." His gaze moved back to hers and he saw the concern and the hurt there. Dammit, he did not want to hurt her. Maddox had done that well enough himself, but she would never know it. "Will you help me or not?"

She tilted up that determined little chin and glared at him, a new flash of anger chasing away the doubt. "And if I refuse, what then?"

"People will die."

She blinked, but to her credit she didn't back off. "So I've heard. Can you be more specific? I need to know what I'm getting into here." Her compact little body literally strummed with her building tension.

The question kind of pissed him off. Or maybe it was the glaring fact that he couldn't keep his mind off her every reaction, couldn't stay focused. "You know, Doc, according to Director Calder, you generally don't question his requests. I understand this is personal," he growled, "but do you really think Maddox would have a problem with me borrowing his face for a little while?"

Her fists clenched and Hennessey had the distinct feeling that it was all she could do not to slap him. Good. He wanted her responses to be real, wanted to clear the air here and now. He didn't need her hesitation coming back to bite him in the ass down the line.

"David would probably say it's the right thing to do," she said tightly. "It's me who has the problem."

He resisted the urge to roll his eyes at her misplaced loyalty. He couldn't help wondering if, when he died, anyone would think so highly of him. Not very damned likely. He was far too open to lead anyone that far off track. Well, except for his targets and that was his job.

In his personal life he kept things on the up-and-up. He never lied to anyone, most especially a woman.

He liked women. Before he could put the brakes on the urge, his gaze roamed down the length of her toned body, admiring those feminine curves, before sliding back up to that madder-than-hell expression on her pretty face.

He liked women a lot. They knew what they were getting with him. If he and the doc did the deed there would be no questions or doubts between them.

But that wasn't going to happen.

Mainly because it would be stupid.

Not to mention the fact that she looked ready to take off his head and spit down his throat.

Fine. If she wanted to play hardball, he was game. "You want to know specifics?" He leaned closer, so close he could see the tiny flecks of gold in those glittering green eyes. "You've completed makeovers on fourteen operatives in the past thirty months. Two of those operatives are dead." One being the man who taught him everything he knew, but he didn't mention that. He had no intention of giving her any personal ammunition. In addition, holding on to control was far too important for him to let his personal issues with this mission get a grip right now. He kept those feelings tightly compartmentalized for a later time. "If I don't stop these guys the rest of those operatives will end up dead as well."

"That's…that's impossible," she stammered, some of the fight going out of her. "How could they know who and where these people are? Who has access to that information?" Her gaze dropped to his lips but quickly jerked back up to his eyes. She looked startled that she had allowed the weakness.

Hennessey laughed softly, allowing his warm breath to feather across those luscious lips. Damn, he was enjoying this far too much. Maybe he should just cut loose and say what was on his mind. That he would do this with or without her help, but that if she had a couple of hours he would show her what she was missing if she really wanted to know how well he lived up to his infamous reputation.

Dumb, Hennessey. Focus. Apparently she was experiencing almost as much trouble as he was.

In answer to her question, he tossed her a response she was not going to like. "You want to know who has access to those names and faces? Directors Calder and Allen, of course, the president, your former boyfriend, me and *you*." He said the last with just as much accusation as she'd thrown at him earlier.

She shuddered visibly, inhaled sharply, the sound doing strange things to his gut, making him even angrier or something along those lines. "Could someone else have gained access to the files?" she demanded, hysteria climbing in her voice.

He shook his head slowly and prepared to deliver the final blow. "Not a chance. Since Maddox is dead and, well, the president is the president, I'd say that narrows down the suspect list to the two directors outside that door." He hitched his thumb in that direction. "And you and me."

Fury whipped across her face, turning those green eyes to the color of smoldering jade. "If you think this tactic is going to pressure me into a yes, you're sadly mistaken, Agent Hennessey."

"Suit yourself." He straightened, a muscle in his cheek jerking as he clenched his jaw so hard his teeth should have cracked. It took a full minute for him to grab back some semblance of control. "Then consider this, *Dr. Cameron.*" He glared down at her, his own fury way beyond reining in now. "If you don't do this most likely my mission will fail, then those operatives will eventually be found and murdered, one by one."

She held her ground, refused to look away though he knew just how lethal his glare could be. "You said two are already dead?" she asked. Her voice quavered just a little.

"That's right," he ground out, ignoring the twinge of regret that pricked him for pushing the jerk routine this far. "And so are their families." He fought the emotion that tightened his throat. He would not let her see the weakness. "You see, Doc, these people aren't happy with just wiping out the list of agents who've gone against what they believe in, they play extra dirty. They kill the family first, making the agent watch, and then they kill the agent, slowly, painfully."

Her eyes grew wider with each word. The pulse fluttered wildly at the base of her throat. She didn't want to hear this, didn't want to know. Too bad. It was the only way.

"So, it's your choice," he went on grimly. "You can either help me stop them or you can try to sleep at night while wondering when the next agent will be located and murdered."

She did turn away this time. Hennessey took a deep breath and cursed himself for being such an idiot. Saying all that hadn't been necessary. But, on some level, he'd wanted to rattle her—to hurt her. He wanted to get to her when the truth was she'd already gotten to him. He'd lost control by steady increments from the moment the director ordered him to start watching her weeks ago.

He had to get back on track here, had to keep those damned personal issues out of this. If the director got even a whiff of how he really felt, he would be replaced. Hennessey couldn't let that happen. He had to do this for a couple of reasons. "I shouldn't have told you," he said, regret slipping into his voice. As much as he'd needed her cooperation, he'd gone too far.

When she turned back to him once more, her face had been wiped clean of emotion, and her analytical side was back. The doctor persona was in place. The woman who could go into an operating room and reconstruct a face damaged so badly that the patient's own family couldn't identify her. No wonder she walked around as cold as ice most of the time. It took nerves of steel and the ability to set her emotions aside to do what she did.

He should respect that.

He did.

It was his other reactions that disturbed him.

"What do you want from me?"

The request unnerved him at a level that startled him all over again.

He focused on the question, denying the uncharacteristic emotions twisting inside him. "I need you to do your magic, Doc." His gaze settled heavily onto hers. "And I need you to work with me. You knew Maddox intimately. Help me become him… just for a little while. Long enough to survive this mission. Long enough to do what has to be done."

For three long beats she said nothing at all. Just when he was certain she would simply walk away, she spoke. "All right." She rubbed at her forehead as if an ache had begun there, then sighed. "On one condition." She looked straight at him.

The intensity…the electricity crackled between them like embers in a building fire. She had to feel it. The lure was very nearly irresistible.

"Name it," he shot back.

"When this is over, I give you back your face. I don't want you being *you* with David's face."

He wanted to pretend the words didn't affect him…but they did. He'd be damned if he'd let her see just how much impact her opinion carried. "I wouldn't have it any other way," he insisted.

"Then we have a deal, Agent Hennessey. When do we start?"

Chapter Four

Elizabeth sat in her car as the purple and gray hues of dawn stole across the sky, chasing away the darkness, ushering forth the new day.

She'd managed a few hours sleep last night but just barely. Her mind kept playing moments spent with David, fleeting images of a past that had, at the time, felt like the beginning of the rest of her life.

How could she have been so foolish as to take that risk? She had known that a relationship with a man like David was an emotional gamble, but she'd dived in headfirst. The move had been so unlike her. She'd spent her entire life carefully calculating her every step.

She'd known by age twelve that she wanted to be a doctor, she just hadn't known what field. As a teenager, pediatrics had appealed to her, in particular helping children with the kind of diseases that robbed them of their youth and dreams. But at nineteen her college roommate had been in a horrifying automobile accident and the weeks and months that followed had brought Elizabeth's future into keen focus as nothing else could have.

Watching her friend go from a vibrant, happy young woman with a brilliant future ahead of her to a shell of a human being with a face that would never be her own had made Elizabeth yearn to prevent that from ever happening again…to anyone.

She'd worked harder than ever, had thrown herself into her education and eventually into her work. That burning desire to do the impossible, to rebuild the single most individual part of the human body, had driven her like a woman obsessed.

Elizabeth sighed. And maybe she was obsessed. If so, she had no hope of making it right because this was who she was, what she did. She made no excuses.

She dragged the keys from her ignition and dropped them into her purse.

But this was different.

Though she had changed faces for the CIA before, a fact for which she had no regrets, this was so *very* different.

Elizabeth emerged from her Lexus, closed the door and automatically depressed the lock button on the remote. The headlights flashed, signaling the vehicle was now secure.

She inhaled a deep breath of the thick August air. It wasn't entirely daylight yet and already she could almost taste the humidity.

"Might as well get this done," she murmured as she shoved her glasses up the bridge of her nose and then trudged across the parking lot.

The CIA had leased, confiscated or borrowed a private clinic for this Saturday morning's procedure. She noted the other vehicles there and, though she recognized none of them, assumed it was the usual team she worked with on these secret procedures. Of course, she would prefer her own team, but the group provided by the CIA in the past were excellent and, admittedly, a sort of rhythm had developed after more than a dozen surgeries.

A guard waited at the side entrance. His appearance made her think of the Secret Service agents who served as bodyguards for the president.

"Good morning, Dr. Cameron," he said as she neared. Though she didn't know him, he obviously knew her. No surprise.

"Morning."

He opened the door for her and she moved inside. It wasn't necessary to ask where the others would be, that part was always the same. Most clinics were set up on a similar floor plan. This one, an upscale cosmetic surgery outpost for the socially elite, was no different in that respect. The plush carpeting rather than the utilitarian tile and lavishly framed pieces of art that highlighted the warm, sand-colored walls were a definite step up from the norm but the basic layout was the same.

Agent Dawson stepped into the hall from one of the examination rooms lining the elegant corridor. "The team is ready when you are, Dr. Cameron."

"Thank you, Agent Dawson." Elizabeth didn't bother dredging up a perfunctory smile. He knew she didn't like this. She sensed that he didn't either. But they both had a duty to do. An obligation to do their part to keep the world as safe as possible. She had to remember that.

The prep room was quiet and deserted and she was glad. She wanted to do this without exchanging any sort of chitchat with those involved, most especially the patient.

As she unbuttoned and dragged off her blouse in one of the private dressing rooms, glimpses of those no-longer-welcome flickers of memory filtered through her mind once more. The last time she'd undressed for David. The last time they'd kissed or made love.

So long ago. Months. Far more than the two he'd been dead.

Her fingers drifted down to her waist and she unzipped her slacks, stepped out of her flats and tugged them off. The question that had haunted her for months before David had died, nagged at her now.

Had he found someone else?

Was that the reason for the tension she'd felt in him the past few times they were together?

Would she ever know how he'd died? Heart attack? Didn't seem feasible considering his excellent health, but healthy men dropped dead all the time. Or had he been killed in the line of duty?

She shook off the memories, forced them back into that little rarely visited compartment where they belonged. She did not want to think about David anymore, didn't want to deconstruct and analyze over and over those final months they had spent together.

None of it mattered now.

After slipping on sterile scrubs, cap and shoe covers and then washing up, she headed to the O.R. where the team would be waiting.

More of those polite and pleasant good-mornings were tossed her way as she entered the well-lit, shiny operating room. One quick sweep told her that the equipment was cutting edge. Nothing but the best.

But then it was always that way. The CIA would choose nothing less for their most important assets.

"He refused to allow us to prepare him for anesthesia until you arrived, Doctor," the anesthesiologist remarked, what she could see of his expression behind the mask reflecting impatience.

"Hey, Doc."

The insolent voice dragged Elizabeth's gaze to the patient. "Good morning, Agent Hennessey." As she spoke, a nurse moved up next to Elizabeth and assisted with sliding her hands into a pair of surgical gloves.

"I think this crew is ready for me to go night-night," Hennessey said in that same flirtatious, roguish tone. "But I wanted to have a final word with you first."

With her mask in place, Elizabeth moved over to the table where Agent Hennessey lay, nude, save for the paper surgical gown and blanket. She frowned as she considered that even now he didn't look vulnerable. This was a moment in a person's life when they generally appeared acutely helpless. But not this man. No, she decided, he possessed far too much ego to feel remotely vulnerable even now as he lay prepared for an elective surgical procedure that could, if any one of a hundred or more things went wrong, kill him.

Those unrepentant blue eyes gleamed as he stared up at her. "Any chance I could have a moment alone with you?" he asked quietly before glancing around at the four other scrub-clad members of her team.

Elizabeth nodded to the anesthesiologist. He, as well as the two physicians and the nurse, stepped to the far side of the room.

"What is it you'd like to say, Agent Hennessey?" she asked, her own impatience making an appearance.

"Look, Doc—" he raised up enough to brace on his elbows "—I know you didn't really want to do this." His eyes searched hers a moment. "But I want you to know how much I appreciate your decision in my favor. I feel a hell of a lot better about this with you here."

She couldn't say just then what possessed her but Elizabeth did something she hadn't done in a very long time, she said exactly what she was thinking rather than the proper thing. "Agent Hennessey, my decision had nothing to do with you. I'm doing this for my country…for those agents who might lose their life otherwise. But I'm definitely not doing this for you."

Looking away, uninterested in his reaction, she motioned for the others to return.

"Let's get this over with," she said crisply.

The team, people whose real names she would likely never know, moved into position, slipped into that instinctive rhythm that would guide them through the process of altering a human face. As the anesthesia did its work Agent Hennessey's eyelids grew heavy, but his gaze never left Elizabeth. He watched her every move.

In that final moment before the blackness sucked him into unconsciousness, his gaze met hers one last time and she saw the faintest glimmer of vulnerability. Elizabeth's heart skipped at the intensity of what was surely no more than a fraction of a second. And then she knew one tiny truth about Agent Joe Hennessey.

He was afraid. Perhaps only a little, but the fear had been there all the same.

Elizabeth steeled herself against the instant regret she experienced at having been so indifferent to his feelings. She doubted he would have wasted the emotion on her, but there it was.

Banishing all other thought she took a deep breath and considered his face. Not Joe Hennessey's face, but the face of her patient. If she allowed herself to think of the patient as an individual just now then she would be more prone to mistakes related to human emotion. This had to be about the work…had to be about planes and angles, sections of flesh and plotting of modifications.

For this procedure she needed no mold, not even a picture. She knew by heart the face she needed to create. The face of the first man she'd ever loved. The only man actually. She'd been far too busy with her education and then her career for a real social life.

"Scalpel," she said as she held out her hand.

With the first incision Elizabeth lost herself in the procedure. No more thoughts of anything past, present or future. Only the work. Only the goal of creating a certain look…a face that was as familiar to her as her own.

ELIZABETH STRIPPED OFF her gloves, quickly scrubbed her hands and then shed the rest of the surgical attire. She cleaned her glasses and shoved them back onto her face.

Exhaustion weighed on her but she ignored it. When she'd donned a fresh, sterile outfit she went in search of coffee. Breakfast had been a while ago and she needed a caffeine jolt.

A cleanup team had already arrived to scrub and sterilize the O.R. Not a trace of the patient would be left behind. It was a CIA thing. Elizabeth knew for a certainty that the clinic would have its own personnel for that very procedure that would be repeated before business hours began on Monday, but the CIA took no chances. Nothing, not a single strand of DNA, that could connect Joe Hennessey to this clinic would be left behind.

For now he was in the recovery room with the nurse and one of the assisting physicians.

Elizabeth sat down in the lounge with a steaming cup of coffee. Thankfully Agent Dawson had a knack with coffee. A box of pastries sat next to the coffeepot. She forced herself to eat a glazed donut when she wasn't particularly hungry, just tired.

Dawson had explained that as soon as Elizabeth considered Hennessey able to move they would relocate via a borrowed ambulance to a safe house. She would oversee his recovery for the next three weeks, ensuring that nothing went wrong. Meanwhile some of the agents whose faces she'd already changed were in hiding, unable to move forward into whatever missions they had been assigned until it was safe for them to return to duty. Some, however, were already deep into missions. Their safety could not be assured without risking the mission entirely.

Her cruise had been cancelled and an additional week of leave had been approved. Director Calder had assured her that the Agency would reimburse her loss which was most of the cost of the cruise. No surprise there. Canceling this close to sail date came with certain drawbacks.

When Elizabeth felt the sugar and caffeine kicking in she pushed up from the table and headed to recovery to check on her patient.

In the corridor Agent Dawson waited for her. "You holding up all right, Dr. Cameron?"

She suppressed the biting retort that came instantly to mind. Dawson didn't deserve the brunt of her irritation. The problem actually lay with her. She'd fallen in love with the wrong man. Had assumed the fairy tale of marriage and family would be hers someday. Two mistakes that were all her own. This particular favor for the CIA had simply driven that point home all over again.

"I'm fine, Agent Dawson."

He nodded. "Agent Hennessey can be a bit brash," he said, his gaze not meeting hers. "But he's the best we have, ma'am. He won't let our people down. He'll get the job done or die trying."

Elizabeth blinked. It was, incredibly, the first time she'd considered that Hennessey might actually lose his life while carrying out this assignment. Clearly, she should have. The business of field operations was hazardous to say the least. David had explained that to her when he'd opted to go back into the field after their relationship had turned personal. She'd tried to talk him out of the change, but he'd been determined and she'd been in love.

End of story.

"I'm glad we can count on him," she said to Dawson, somehow mustering up a smile.

"The transportation for moving to the safe house is ready whenever you are, Doctor Cameron."

She nodded and continued on toward recovery. This was the first time she and Dawson had suffered any tension. The meetings with him were generally brief and superficial. This intensity was uncomfortable. Just something else to dislike about this situation.

As she pushed through the double doors the nurse looked up and smiled. "His vitals are stable, Doctor."

Elizabeth nodded. "Excellent."

She moved to the table and surveyed the sleeping patient and the various readouts providing continual information as to his status.

Heart rate was strong and steady. Respiration deep and regular.

The bandages hiding his incisions wouldn't be coming off for a few days. Even then the redness and swelling would still be prominent. After three weeks the worst would have passed. His age and excellent state of good health helped in the healing.

With some patients, especially older ones, some minor swelling and redness persisted for weeks, even months after extensive surgery. But there was no reason to believe that would be the case with this patient. The work Elizabeth had done was more about rearranging and sculpting, no deep tissue restructuring or skeletal changes. Minor alterations had been made to his nose and chin using plastic implants. Those would later be removed when she returned his face to its natural look. There would be minor scarring that she'd carefully hidden in hollows and angles. Fortunately for him his skin type and coloring generally scarred very little.

Later as Elizabeth sat alone in recovery, her patient started to rouse. The nurse and assisting physician had, at her urging, retired to the lounge. Both had looked haggard and ready for a break. She'd seen no reason, considering the continued stability of the patient's vitals, for all of them to stay with him.

Now she wished she wasn't alone. Her trepidation was unwarranted, she knew, but some part of her worried that she might see more of that vulnerability and she did not want to feel sympathy for this man. Now or ever.

He licked his lips. Made a sound in his throat. The intubation tube left patients with a dry throat. His right hand moved ever so slightly then jerked as some part of him recognized that he was restrained.

His body grew rigid then restless.

Stepping closer Elizabeth lay her hand on his arm and spoke quietly to him. "Agent Hennessey, you're waking up from anesthesia now. The surgery went well. There is no reason to be apprehensive."

His lids struggled to open as he continued to thrash just a little against his restraints.

"Agent Hennessey, can you hear me?"

He moistened his lips again and tried to speak.

Instinctively Elizabeth's hand moved down to his. "You can open your eyes, Agent Hennessey, you're doing fine."

His fingers curled around hers and her breath caught.

Blue eyes stared up at her then, the pupils dilated with the remnants of the drugs his body worked hard to metabolize and flush away.

"Everything is fine, Agent Hennessey."

"I guess I survived the knife, Doc," he said, his voice rusty.

An unexpected smile tilted her lips. "You did, indeed. We'll be moving to the safe house shortly."

"Any chance I could have a drink?" he asked with another swipe of his tongue over his lips.

"Certainly." It wasn't until then that Elizabeth noticed that his fingers were still closed tightly around hers. She wiggled free and poured some cool water into a cup. When she'd inserted a bendable straw she held the tip to his lips so that he could drink. "Not too much," she warned, but, of course, like all other patients he didn't listen. She had to take the straw away before he'd stopped.

She wiped his lips with a damp cloth. "For the first few days we'll keep the pain meds flowing for your comfort," she said, all too aware of the silence.

He mumbled something that might have been *whatever you think, Doc.*

A few hours later, most of which Agent Hennessey had slept through, Elizabeth supervised his movement to the waiting ambulance. She had learned that her determination of when the patient was ready to be moved had less to do with their departure than the arrival of darkness. Made sense when she thought about it. Night provided good cover.

"I'll be riding in the front with the driver," Dawson explained. "The nurse will accompany you to the safe house for the night. Tomorrow his care will be solely in your hands as long as you feel additional help is no longer required."

Elizabeth felt confident that additional medical support wouldn't be necessary, but she couldn't say that she looked forward to spending time alone with Hennessey. What she had done to alter his face was only the beginning of what Director Calder expected of her.

She settled onto the gurney opposite Agent Hennessey and considered the rest of this assignment. It was her job to ensure that this man could walk, talk and display mannerisms matching those of David Maddox.

Elizabeth knew nothing of David's work, but she did know the things he talked about when off duty... when in her bed.

"Feels like we're moving."

Elizabeth stared down at the man strapped to the other gurney. His mouth and eyes were all that was visible but his voice, the cocky tone that screamed of his arrogant attitude, made him easily recognizable.

"We're on our way to the safe house," she explained. He knew the plan, but the lingering effects of anesthesia and the newly introduced pain medication were playing havoc with his ability to concentrate.

"So I get to spend my first night with you, huh?"

A blush heated her cheeks. Though she doubted Agent Hennessey felt any real discomfort just now, she could not believe he had the audacity to flirt with her.

"In a manner of speaking," she said calmly. The man could very well be feeling a bit loose-tongued. He might not mean to flirt.

He made a sound in his chest, a laugh perhaps. "I've been dying to get you all to myself ever since that night," he mumbled.

Taken aback, Elizabeth reminded herself that he probably wouldn't even remember anything he said. Ignoring the remark was likely the best course.

"Sorry," he muttered. "I didn't mean to let that slip out."

She'd suspected as much. Swiping her hands on her thighs she sat back, relaxed her shoulders against the empty shelves behind her. "That's all right, Agent Hennessey," she allowed, "most patients say more than they mean to when on heavy-duty painkillers."

He licked his lips and groaned. The doctor in her went on immediate alert. "Are you feeling pain now, Agent Hennessey?" Surely not. He'd been dosed half an hour prior to their departure.

He inhaled a big breath. "No way, Doc, I'm flying over here." He blinked a few times then turned his head slowly to look at her. "God, you're gorgeous, did you know that?"

Elizabeth sat a little straighter, tugged at the collar of her blouse to occupy her hands. "You might want to get some more sleep, Hennessey, before you say something you'll regret."

"Too late, right?" He made another of those rumbling sounds that were likely an attempt at chuckling. "No big deal." He waved a hand dismissively. "You already know how gorgeous you are."

Maybe his hands should have been restrained. He'd been secured to ensure he didn't roll off the gurney, but his arms had been left free.

"You should lay still, Agent—"

"Yeah, yeah, I know," he interrupted. "Don't move, don't say anything. That's what I do best. But at least I'd never lie to you like he did. Never…" His eyes closed reluctantly as if the drugs had belatedly kicked in and he couldn't keep them open any longer.

Elizabeth let go a breath of relief. She checked his pulse and relaxed a little more when it appeared he'd drifted back to sleep.

Lending any credence to anything he'd said was ridiculous under the circumstances. The drugs had him confused and talking out of his head. She knew that, had seen it numerous times.

But the part about lying wouldn't let her put his ramblings out of her mind. What did he mean by that remark?

Nothing, you fool, she scolded.

She folded her arms over her chest. Then why did it feel familiar? As if he'd said what she'd thought a dozen times over. Because she'd sensed that David had been lying to her for quite some time.

Elizabeth closed her eyes and chastised herself for going down that road. David was dead. Whatever he'd said to her, lies or not, no longer mattered. He wasn't coming back. He was gone forever.

Dead.

She opened her eyes and stared at the bandaged face of the man lying so still less than two feet from her. Nothing he told her would matter. She'd loved David. He was gone. She wouldn't be taking that rocky route again anytime soon.

Nothing that Agent Joe Hennessey said or did would alter her new course.

As soon as this was over she intended to revive her social life as planned. Start dating again.

It was past time.

Chapter Five

Joe studied his reflection for far longer than the bandaged mug warranted. He didn't know what he expected to see or what it mattered. The deed was done.

Twenty-four hours had passed since he'd gone under the knife. He pretty much felt like hell. His whole head could be a puffy melon if it weren't for the pain radiating around his face in ever tightening bands coming to a point at his nose. He'd had his nose broken once, but it hadn't hurt like this.

He glanced at the table next to his bed. There was medication for the pain, except he preferred to put off taking it until the pain became intolerable.

So far this morning, he had avoided spending much time with the doc. He'd been aware of her coming in and out of his room all during the night to check the portable monitors that provided a continuous scorecard on his vitals. He'd felt her looking at him each time but he hadn't opened his eyes, hadn't wanted to talk to her. He had a bad feeling he'd already said too much.

That was part of the reason he had no intention of taking any more drugs than necessary. He vaguely recalled making a few ridiculous remarks in the ambulance on the way here.

Joe exhaled a heavy breath. He was thirty-eight years old. He'd been an undercover operative for the CIA for the past ten. He'd been tortured, subjected to all sorts of training to prepare him for said torture, and not once had he ever spilled his guts like he almost had yesterday.

"Real stupid, Hennessey."

He dragged on his shirt and decided he couldn't hide out in this room any longer. It was 9:00 a.m. and his need for caffeine wouldn't be ignored any longer.

Facing the enemy had never been a problem for him. Hiding out from the doc when she was supposed to be on his side bordered on cowardice.

Joe hesitated at the door. He could admit that. It was the truth after all. Why would he lie to himself? The next three weeks were a part of the mission. He'd simply have to get past his personal feelings. Too many lives hung in the balance for him to indulge his personal interests.

His fingers wrapped around the doorknob and he twisted, drew back the door and exited the room that provided some amount of separation. All he had to do was maintain his boundaries. No slipping into intimate territory in conversation. No touching. If he followed those two simple rules he wouldn't have a problem.

The upstairs hall stretched fifteen yards from the room he'd just exited to the staircase. Three other bedrooms and two bathrooms had been carved out of the space. Downstairs was more or less one large open space that served as living room, kitchen and dining room. A laundry room with rear exit, pantry and half bath were off the kitchen.

The house was located in the fringes of a small Maryland town. There was only one other house on the street and it was currently vacant and for sale. Twenty-four hour surveillance as well as a state-of-the-art security system ensured their safety. A panic room had been installed in the basement. Even if someone got past surveillance and the security system they wouldn't breach the panic room. Though only twelve-by-twelve, the room was impenetrable and stocked for every imaginable scenario.

The smooth hardwood of the stair treads felt cold beneath Joe's bare feet. His left hand slid along the banister as he descended to the first floor, the act taking him back a few decades to his childhood. His parents' home had been a two-story and he and his brother had traveled down the stairs every imaginable way from sliding down the banister to jumping over it. It was a miracle either one of them had survived boyhood.

Joe stopped on the bottom step and hesitated once more before making his presence known.

Doctor Elizabeth Cameron was busy at the sink, filling the carafe to make another pot of coffee Joe presumed. A glutton for punishment he stood there and watched, unable to help himself.

She'd traded her usual businesslike attire for jeans and a casual blouse. He hadn't seen her like this. She wore generic sweats when she worked out, her scrubs or a business suit including a conservative skirt or slacks the rest of the time. He'd begun to wonder as he watched her over the past couple of weeks if she slept in her work clothes. Her cool, reserved exterior just didn't lend itself to the idea of silky lingerie no matter how much she owned.

And yet, when his gaze followed the sweet curves of her body clearly delineated by the form-fitting blue jeans and pale pink top he found himself ready to amend that conclusion.

At about five-four, she would fit neatly into the category of petite without question, but she was strong. He'd watched her work out. She could run like hell. More than once he'd wished she would wear shorts for her workouts rather than sweatpants, but he never got that lucky. He liked it a lot when she took off those unflattering glasses, which was extremely rare.

Just then she turned around, spotted him and jumped. Her hand flew to her chest. "You scared me!"

He took the final step down as she caught her breath. "Sorry." And he was, but not about startling her. He was sorry she'd caught him watching her like that. The last thing he needed was her putting together his loopy comments in the ambulance and his gawking this morning and coming up with the idea that he liked her in ways he shouldn't.

"I was just making a fresh pot of coffee." She gestured with the carafe. "There's eggs, bacon and toast. It was delivered about fifteen minutes ago."

While he was in the shower. Apparently Director Calder didn't want the good doctor to have to concern herself with preparing meals. Joe's reputation for lousy cuisine had apparently preceded him.

"Great." He crossed the room. The closer he got the more her hand shook as she poured the water into the coffeemaker. The idea that he made her nervous intrigued him just a little, though it shouldn't. He imagined she was still annoyed about his manhandling three months ago.

"I hope you like it strong," she commented without looking at him as she shoved the empty carafe under the drip basket. "At the hospital we prefer it with enough kick to keep us going."

He stopped three feet away, leaned against the counter. "That's the only way I drink it."

She glanced up at him and pushed a smile into place with visible effort. "How do you feel this morning?" Her gaze examined the bandages.

"Like hell," he admitted. "You didn't take a baseball bat to my head while I slept last night, did you?"

Worry lined her smooth complexion. "The pain meds should alleviate most of the discomfort."

Lured by the scent of the brewing coffee, he reached for a mug. She stiffened as his arm brushed her shoulder. "I guess if I took two like you ordered, they might," he confessed.

She rolled her eyes and huffed out a breath of frustration. "Men. You're all the same. You think taking pain medication makes you look like a wimp. That is so silly. The more pain you tolerate the more adrenaline your body will produce to help you cope. The more adrenaline pumping the less effective the medication you actually do take."

"Sounds like a vicious cycle, Doc." He set the mug on the counter. His gut rumbled. "Speaking of vicious." He glanced at the foam containers. "I'm starved." He'd had juice and water yesterday. A little soup last night but definitely not enough for a guy accustomed to packing away the groceries.

"You see," she snapped. "That's my point exactly."

He turned back to her. She'd folded her arms over her chest and now glared at him through those too clunky glasses. Somehow he'd pissed her off.

"What?" he asked in the humblest tone he possessed.

"You just ignored what I said." She gestured to his bandaged face. "You've been through extensive surgery and would still be in the hospital if you were one of my *real* patients. Yet you ignore my orders regarding meds. There are reasons the medication is prescribed, Agent Hennessey. What don't you understand about the process?"

Okay, calm down, Elizabeth ordered the side of her that wanted to obsess on the subject. She'd let him get to her already and he'd scarcely entered the room. She took a deep breath, tried to slow her racing heart. How did he do this to her just walking into the room?

"Look, Doc." He leaned against the counter next to her again. "I'm not trying to be cranky. I took the antibiotics. I even took the pain killer, but only one, not two. That dosage dulls my senses. And I need my senses sharp."

Though, arguably, she could see the logic in what he said, he needed to see hers as well. They were going to be here together for three long weeks. Taking a couple of days to get past the worst of the pain from surgery wasn't too much to ask in her opinion.

"Agent Hennessey," she began with as much patience as she could summon, "it wouldn't kill you to take an additional forty-eight hours of complete downtime."

He reached around her for the coffee, taking her breath for a second time with his nearness. She hated that he possessed that kind of power over her. Men like him should come with a warning. Don't get too close. She knew the hazards, had learned them firsthand with David. And David had been a kitty cat compared to this guy. Hennessey's unmarred record for getting the job done wasn't the only thing for which he had a reputation.

He poured himself a cup of coffee then started to put the carafe away. Elizabeth quickly scooted out of his path to avoid another close encounter.

"Trust me, Doc," he said before taking a sip of his coffee. The groan of satisfaction was another of those things she could have done without. "I'll be the first to admit it if I can't handle the pain without the second pill every four hours. Deal?"

The last time she'd agreed to a deal with him it had landed her here. But then, like him, she had a job to do. People to protect. And maybe that made her an adrenaline junkie, too, although she didn't think so. Sure, her work for the CIA was covert to a degree, but she only saw it as doing her part. It wasn't much but it was something.

Did men like Joe Hennessey look at "their part" the same way? She just didn't know. Figuring out what made him tick wasn't on her agenda. She'd thought she had David all figured out and she'd been wrong and they'd shared thoughts as well as bodily fluids for more than a year. What could she possibly expect to learn about this man in a mere three weeks?

Nothing useful.

Nothing that would add to the quality of her life or give closure to her past.

Considering those two cold hard facts, her best course of action was to steer clear of emotional entanglement in this situation.

"All right, Agent Hennessey," she agreed reluctantly. "You're correct. You are a grown man. The level of pain you can and are willing to tolerate is your call. Just make sure you take the antibiotics as directed." She looked him square in the eyes. "That part is *my* call."

"Yes, ma'am." The wink immediately obliterated any hope of sincerity in his answer.

She had to get her mind off him. Her gaze landed on the breakfast another agent had delivered. Food was as good a distraction as any. Hennessey had said he was hungry.

Each container was laden with oodles of cholesterol and enough calories to fuel an entire soccer team through at least one game. Hennessey didn't hesitate. He dug in as if he hadn't eaten in a month. But his enthusiasm waned when the chewing action elicited a new onslaught of pain.

"Sure you don't want that full dosage?" she asked casually. It wasn't that she enjoyed knowing he was in more pain than he wanted to admit, but being right did carry its own kind of glee.

"I'm fine."

She didn't particularly like the idea that her unnecessary remark only made him more determined to continue without the aid of additional medication. Maybe she shouldn't have said anything at all.

While she picked at the eggs, sausage and biscuits on her plate, he ate steadily, however slowly. Oatmeal or yogurt would have been a much better choice. She wondered if he'd been the one to order the food. There hadn't been any calls in or out. Or perhaps the agent just picked up for them whatever he'd picked up for himself.

Checking on the menu for the next few days might be a good idea.

Elizabeth dropped her fork to her plate. Why had she done this? Why wasn't she on that cruise? She could have said no. That wasn't true.

People will die.

Saying no actually hadn't been an option.

"Agent Hennessey."

He met her gaze. "Yeah?"

As much as he tried to hide it she didn't miss the dull look that accompanied the endurance of significant pain.

She sighed and set her food aside. "Look, let's not play this game. You're obviously in pain. I would really feel a lot better if you took your medication."

"I told you I'm fine."

The words had no more left his lips than he bolted from the table and headed for the short corridor beyond the kitchen that led to the laundry room and downstairs bathroom.

Instinctively, Elizabeth followed. His violent

heaves told on him before she caught sight of him kneeling at the toilet.

He'd been pushing the limits ever since he regained his equilibrium after anesthesia. This was bound to happen.

Ignoring the unpleasant sounds she moved to the wash basin next to him and moistened a washcloth. When he'd flushed the toilet and managed to get to his feet, she passed the damp cloth to him.

"I think you should be in bed."

"You know what, Doc? I think you're right."

Unbelievable. What was most incredible was that he didn't try to turn her words into something lewd or suggestive.

She followed him up the stairs and into the room he'd used the night before. He climbed between the sheets without putting up a fuss. To her surprise he even took the other pain pill she offered without argument.

"Thanks," he mumbled, his eyes closed.

When Elizabeth would have moved away from the bed his fingers curled around her wrist and held on. "What's the rush, Doc?" He tugged her down onto the side of the bed next to him.

She tried to relax but couldn't. "You should rest."

"I'm lying flat on my back. I've taken the pills. At least give me this."

If he hadn't looked at her so pleadingly, she might have been able to refuse. But there was that glimmer of vulnerability again and she just couldn't do it.

"What is it that you want, Agent Hennessey?"

"First." He moistened those full lips. Strange, she considered, his lips were awfully full for a man's. There hadn't been a lot she could do about that. The best they could hope for was that no one would notice. "I'd like you to stop calling me Agent Hennessey. Call me Joe."

His fingers still hung around her wrist, more loosely now, but the contact was there. Pulling away would have been a simple matter but he was her patient and she needed him to relax. So she didn't pull away.

"All right, Joe," she complied. "I suppose then that you should call me Elizabeth." Most anything was preferable to Doc. Although she did have to admit that he somehow made it sound sexy.

He licked his lips and said her name, "Elizabeth. It suits you."

She wasn't sure whether that was a compliment or not, but she decided not to ask.

"Talk to me," he urged, the fingers around her wrist somehow slipping down to entwine with hers.

"Tell me about your relationship with Maddox. What attracted you to him?"

They were supposed to do this. That's why she was here, beyond the surgery that is. She was supposed to make sure he knew about David's personal life—at least as much as she knew. He needed to get the voice down pat and the mannerisms. Practice would accomplish both. But the details were another matter. She had to give him the details just in case David discussed his private life with someone Hennessey—Joe, she amended—might come in contact with during the course of this undercover operation.

Elizabeth saw no point in putting off the inevitable. Getting on with it was the best way.

"He was nice," she said. And it was true. She hadn't known what to expect out of a CIA handler and his being nice was the first thing she was drawn to. All extraneous assets utilized by the CIA were assigned handlers as a go-between. She didn't say because he certainly knew this already.

"Ouch. Maybe you don't know this, honey, but nice is not a man's favorite adjective."

"Elizabeth," she corrected, feeling even more awkward with his use of the endearment though she felt confident he didn't mean it as an actual endearment.

"Elizabeth," he acknowledged.

Even then, as he acquiesced to her assertion he made one of his own. He drew tiny circles on her palm with the pad of his thumb.

She started to pull her hand away, but decided that would only allow him to see that he'd gotten to her. Pretending his little digs at her composure didn't bother her would carry far more weight. When he saw that he couldn't get to her in that way he would surely let it go.

"I liked his jokes," she went on in hopes of losing herself in the past. She worked hard not to do that on a regular basis; doing so now was a stab at keeping her mind off how being this close to Joe Hennessey unnerved her. It shouldn't, but it did.

"Yeah, he was a jokester," Joe murmured.

His voice had thickened a little from the action of the painkiller. If she were lucky he'd fall asleep soon. His body needed the rest. Whether he realized it or not his whole system was working hard to heal his new wounds which diverted strength and energy from other aspects of his existence. He didn't need to fight the process.

Something he'd said in the ambulance, about lying, pinged her memory. She'd have to ask him about that later when he was further along in his recovery.

"So he was nice," Joe reiterated, "and he could tell a joke. Is that why you fell for him?"

His lids had drifted shut now. He wouldn't last much longer. Elizabeth was glad. She stared at their joined hands. Hers smooth and pale, his rougher, far darker as if he spent most of his time on a beach somewhere.

As she watched, his fingers slackened, lay loose between hers. His respiration was deep and slow. She doubted he would hear her answer even if she bothered to give one. But he'd asked, why not respond?

"No, Agent Hennessey, those are not the reasons I fell for him." She paused and when he didn't correct her she knew he was down for the count. "I fell for him because he was like you," she confessed, her voice barely a whisper. "He made me feel things that terrified me and, at the same time, made me feel alive." As hard as she'd tried not to look back and see herself as stupid, she couldn't help it. She'd been so damned foolish.

"And look where it got me," she muttered, annoyed with herself for dredging up the memories.

With every intention of leaving the room she started to pull her hand from the big, warm cradle of his and his fingers abruptly closed firmly around hers.

"Don't stop now, Elizabeth," he murmured without opening his eyes. "You're just getting to the good part."

The only thing that kept her from slapping him was the fact that she would likely undo some of her handiwork and have to do it all over again.

Instead, she held her fury in check and went on as if he'd misinterpreted what she'd said. Tomorrow, or even after that, if he questioned her about her comment she would lie through her teeth and swear she hadn't said any such thing. Two could play this game, she decided.

Stating the facts as if they described someone else's life she told Joe Hennessey the story of how Agent David Maddox had come into her life as her handler and proceeded to lure her into temptation with his vast charm.

Hennessey would no doubt recognize the story. He probably practiced the same M.O. all the time. According to what David had told her, Hennessey left a heartbroken woman behind at every assignment. He was the proverbial James Bond. The man who had it all. A new secret life, with all it entailed, every week.

How exciting it must be to live that kind of life with absolutely no accountability to anyone. The broken hearts he left behind would certainly be chalked up to collateral damage just as the occasional dead body surely was.

Elizabeth worked hard at keeping her tone even and her temper out of the mix, but it wasn't easy. The more she talked about the past and considered her relationship with David, the more she realized how she hadn't ever really known him. She only knew what had drawn her to him.

She didn't really know David the man. She only knew David the lover.

She knew what he'd allowed her to see.

That realization was the hardest of all.

Her gaze dropped to Joe Hennessey. This time he was definitely sleeping. She couldn't help wondering if he'd done this on purpose. Made her see.

She tugged her hand free of his and admitted yet another painful truth. No. This was no one's fault but her own. She'd seen what she'd wanted to see.

Nothing more.

And now she knew the whole truth.

Her relationship with David had been based on an illusion that she had created in her mind.

Elizabeth left Hennessey's room.

She progressed down the stairs and walked to the front door. She unlocked and opened it and came face-to-face with the agent assigned to that location.

"I need to see Director Calder," she said, her voice lacking any real emotion.

"Is there a problem, Dr. Cameron?" the agent asked, his dark eyewear no doubt concealing an instant concern for the two principals it was his job to protect.

"Yes, there is," she said bluntly. "I need to go home. I've decided I can't complete this assignment. Please call the director for me."

Elizabeth closed the door. There was nothing else to say.

She'd made up her mind.

Agreeing to this part of his mission had been a mistake. Giving someone David's face was one thing but she could not do the rest. There had to be someone else who knew David's personality well enough to help Hennessey grasp the necessary elements. Surely there were videos the CIA had made, tapes of interviews David had conducted.

However they conducted this portion of the mission from here had nothing to do with her.

She wanted out.

Chapter Six

Three days elapsed before Elizabeth would again speak to him about her relationship with Maddox.

Today was his first "official" Maddox lesson. They were finally getting down to business. 'Bout time.

That first night at the safe house she had left him sleeping and called the director. Not the director of field operations. The frigging director of the CIA himself. She had demanded to be taken home, had insisted that she wanted no further part in this operation.

Somehow Director Calder had changed her mind.

Since Joe had slept through the whole thing he had no idea how the director had accomplished the feat.

At any rate, Joe had awakened the next morning to an edict from the good doctor. She refused to discuss anything about the assignment with Joe until three days had passed. She wanted him to stay on the full dosage of the medication and in bed during said time. He hadn't liked it one damned bit, but what choice did he have? It wasn't like he could disobey a direct order from Calder.

During those three days Elizabeth had attended to his medical needs. She'd changed his bandages. Thankfully at this point the bulkier gauze was gone. The swelling was still pretty ugly as was the redness. He looked like he'd been on the losing end of a pool house brawl.

"Not like that," she said, her impatience showing.

"Show me," Joe countered, his own patience thinning.

It wasn't like he'd been around Maddox that much. Getting his mannerisms down pat wasn't going to be easy without a better understanding of how he moved.

Elizabeth did the thing with her right arm that she was convinced Joe would never get right. A clever little salute of a wave Maddox had tossed her way every time he saw her. It wasn't that big a deal. He doubted Maddox waved at his targets.

Since she waited, glaring at him, Joe assumed she was ready for him to try again. So he did.

She shook her head. "That's still not right." At his annoyed look she threw up her hands. "This is impossible! You're not going to get it. You're not him!"

Enough.

Joe got right in her face. She blinked, but to her credit, she didn't back off.

"You know what, you're right, I'm not him." He grappled to regain some kind of hold on his temper. "What I need is for you to teach me what I need to know, not dog out my every attempt."

She held her ground, her arrogant little chin jutting out even further. "You know what? I think we need a break."

He straightened, shook his head. "Oh yeah. That's what we need. We've just gotten started and already we need a break. At this rate all those agents will be dead and we won't even need to go through with this operation anyway."

Her mouth opened and the harsh intake of breath told him he'd hit his mark way before the hurt glimmering in her eyes told the tale. "Someone else is dead?"

Dammit. He hadn't meant to tell her about that. Calder had instructed him to keep quiet about the latest hit for fear she would be so shaken she wouldn't be able to continue with their work. Continue, hell, they hadn't even started. Not really.

He booted her words from the other night out of his head. He couldn't keep going over that like a repeating blog. She'd admitted, when she thought he was asleep, that he affected her and her words had affected him. Even half-comatose he'd felt a surge of want deep in his gut.

Maybe it was just the fact that he'd despised Maddox that made him want her. Then again, the truth was, he hadn't known Maddox that well. Maybe he'd despised Maddox because he had the girl Joe wanted.

And he wouldn't have ever known if it hadn't been for that one night.

That night had changed everything.

"Answer me, Hennessey," she demanded. "Who is dead?"

His hope that being on a first-name basis might bring a unity and informality to their work had bombed big time.

"Agent Motley. You may not remember him—"

"I remember him," she interrupted. "He was the first transformation."

She looked ready to crumple but somehow she didn't. Instead she looked at him with hellfire in her eyes. "What about his family?"

Joe hated even worse to tell her this part. "His wife was murdered as well. But his daughter was away with friends so she's okay."

Elizabeth shook her head. "She isn't okay, Hennessey. She won't ever be okay again. Her parents were murdered and she's alone."

Neither of them moved for five seconds that turned into ten. He couldn't help wondering if the person Elizabeth was really talking about was her. She was alone…basically. Her father, retired Colonel Cameron, had died years ago, but her mother was still alive, at least in body. Alzheimer's had made an invalid of her and she no longer recognized her own daughter. She lived in a home especially for Alzheimer's patients. Maddox had been Elizabeth's only viable emotional attachment.

Was that why she had such trouble dealing with this operation?

"She won't be alone, Elizabeth," Joe said softly. He resisted the urge to move closer, to comfort her with his touch. "She has aunts, uncles and cousins. It won't be the same but she won't be alone."

Elizabeth wet her lips. He saw her lower one tremble just a little. "That's good." She nodded. "I'm glad she has a support system."

The way you didn't? he wanted to ask.

"Who are we really talking about here, Elizabeth? You or Agent Motley's daughter?"

Fury flashed across her face. "I don't know what you mean, Agent Hennessey. I'm perfectly fine."

"I think you haven't gotten over losing Maddox."

Judging by the horror in her eyes, completely deflating her anger, he'd royally screwed up by making that comment.

"This isn't a counseling session, Agent Hennessey," she returned coolly, too coolly. "I don't need your conclusions on my relationships."

"Relationship," he corrected, asking for more trouble.

She glowered at him. "What the hell is that supposed to mean?"

He shrugged. Hell, he was in over his head now, might as well say the rest. "*Relationship,*" he repeated. "From what I can tell that's the only long-term commitment you've been involved in. Before or since."

Her hands settled on her hips, drawing his reluctant attention to the way her jeans molded to her soft curves. Damn, he was doomed.

"Who gave you permission to look into my background? Especially my personal life?" she demanded, her tone stone cold now. She was fighting mad.

"I've been watching you for weeks, *Elizabeth,*" he said, purposely saying her name the way he'd heard Maddox say it on the few times they'd met. "It was part of my job. Get to know your routine. Get to know you. Find out who you talked to. Where you went. What you ate. Who you slept with."

She staggered back a couple of steps. "You've been watching me?"

The question came out as if the reality of what he'd been saying had only just penetrated.

"That's right. I've watched every move you've made for weeks," he replied, stoking the flames with pure fuel.

Her eyes rounded. "I haven't slept with anyone since…" Her words trailed off and something achy and damaged flickered in her eyes. Something he couldn't quite name and never wanted to see again.

"Since Maddox," he finished for her. And then he turned away, unable to look at the emotional wreckage he'd caused. It hadn't been necessary for him to push that hard. He could have stopped this before it went anywhere near this far.

"Try again."

What the hell?

He turned back to her and she stood, arms crossed over her chest, glaring at him. "What?"

"I said," she hurled the words at him, "try again. People are dying. You have to get this right."

Something shifted inside him then, made him wish he could turn back time and do those last few minutes over. He hadn't meant to hurt her but he had. But she was too strong, too determined to let him win without a fight.

Dr. Elizabeth Cameron was no coward.

Just something else to admire about her.

ELIZABETH AWAKENED that night from a frightful nightmare. David had been calling to her, begging her for help and she couldn't reach him. No matter how she'd tried he just appeared to draw farther and farther away.

She tried to get her bearings now. It was completely dark. Not home. The safe house. Joe Hennessey.

A breath whooshed out of her lungs and she relaxed marginally. The dream must have awakened her.

A soft rap sounded from her door and she bolted upright. A dozen probable reasons, all bad, for her being awakened in the middle of the night crashed one by one through her mind. She felt for her glasses on the bedside table. "Yes?"

"Dr. Cameron, this is Agent Stark. We may have a problem."

Elizabeth was out of the bed before the man finished his statement. She dragged on her robe and rushed to the door without bothering with a light.

"What's wrong?" The hall was empty save for Agent Stark. A table lamp some ten feet away back-lit the tall man and his requisite black suit.

"I'm not sure there's a real problem, but Agent Hennessey has requested that we bring in something for stomach cramps. Agent Dawson insisted I check with you first."

Stomach cramps? Worry washed over her. "I'll need my bag."

Stark nodded. "I'll wait for you at Agent Hennessey's room."

Elizabeth flipped on the overhead light and rushed around the room until she determined where she'd left her bag last. She never had this problem at home. But here, with *him,* she felt perpetually out of sorts.

By the time she was in the hall she could hear Hennessey growling at his fellow agent.

"I don't need the doc, Stark. I need something for—"

"Thank you, Agent Stark," Elizabeth said by way of dismissal when she barged, without knocking, into the room. "I'll let you know if we need anything."

Judging by Hennessey's bedcovers he'd been writhing in discomfort for some time. "Why didn't you let me know you needed me?" she demanded of her insubordinate patient.

"I don't need a doctor," he grumped as he sat up. One hand remained fastened against his gut. "What I need is Maalox or Pepto. Something for a stomachache. Apparently dinner disagreed with me."

Before Elizabeth could fathom his intent he stood,

allowing the sheet to fall haphazardly where it would, mostly around his ankles, and leaving him clothed in nothing more than a wrinkled pair of boxers. She looked away but not soon enough. The image of strong, muscled legs and a lean, ribbed waist was already permanently and indelibly imprinted upon at least a dozen brain cells.

"Oh, man." He bent forward slightly in pain.

Elizabeth tried to reconcile the man who refused the proper dose of pain medication with one who couldn't tolerate a few stomach cramps without demanding a remedy.

"Are you sure it was something you ate?" Less than a week had passed since his surgery, there were a number of problems that could crop up. Before he could answer, she added, "Let's have a look."

"Come on, Doc, this isn't necessary," he grumbled.

She held up a hand. "Sit, Agent Hennessey."

With a mighty exhale he collapsed back onto the bed. She didn't really need to see the rest of his face. His eyes said it all. He had no patience for this sort of thing.

When she'd tucked the thermometer into his mouth, she moved to the door and asked Agent Stark to send for an over-the-counter tonic for stomach cramps. He hadn't mentioned any other issues that generally went hand-in-hand with cramps, but she didn't see any reason to take the risk. The medication she requested would cover either or both symptoms.

Hennessey sat on the edge of the bed, the thermometer protruding from his lips, and he looked exactly like a petulant child with an amazingly grown-up body. And a layer of gauze concealing the majority of his face.

She thought of the agent who'd died in the past twenty-four hours and she prayed that her efforts wouldn't be too little too late. She'd taken an oath to save lives. Had her support of the CIA helped or hurt? She had thought her work would save them from this very fate and now it seemed those she had helped were on a list marked for death.

How could that be?

It didn't make sense.

"Normal," she commented aloud after reading the thermometer. She set the old-fashioned instrument on the bedside table next to her bag. "Any other symptoms."

"No." He groaned. "At least not yet."

"Let me have a look at your face." She'd changed his bandages this morning and all had looked well enough. Still some redness and swelling, but that was perfectly normal.

"My face isn't the problem." He pushed her hands away. "It's my gut."

Worry gnawing at her, she reached into her bag and removed her stethoscope and blood pressure cuff. She saw no reason to take chances.

Hennessey swore but she ignored him. BP was only slightly elevated. The thrashing around in the bed and any sort of pain could be responsible for that.

She listened to his heart and lungs. Nothing out of the ordinary. His heart sounded strong and steady.

As she put the cuff and stethoscope away he said, "I told you I was fine."

"Yes, you did," she agreed. "But I would be remiss in my duties if I didn't double-check."

He made a sound that loudly telegraphed his doubt of her motives. "You probably just wanted an excuse to see me in my shorts," he said glibly.

Elizabeth tamped down her first response of annoyance and thought about that remark for a moment. Deciding he wasn't the only one who could throw curves, she sat down beside him. Tension went through him instantly, stiffening his shoulders and making the muscle in his jaw flex.

"Actually, Agent Hennessey, I've already seen most of you the day of surgery." She produced a smile at his narrowed gaze. "Sometimes when they shift a patient from the surgical gurney sheets drop and gowns get shoved up around waists." As true as her statement was, it hadn't happened with him but he didn't have to know that. "But don't worry," she assured him, "the only person who laughed was the nurse, but don't tell her I told you."

Elizabeth would have given anything to see his face just then. If the red rushing up his neck was any indication, his whole face was most likely beet-red.

She couldn't torture him too long. He did have a problem. "I'm kidding, Hennessey."

He moved his head slowly from side to side but didn't look at her. "Very good, Doc, you might get the hang of this after all."

Feeling guilty for her bad joke, she urged him back into bed and tucked the sheet properly around him. Minutes later Stark arrived with the medication. Elizabeth thanked him and gave Hennessey the proper dose.

She settled into the chair near the bedside table and waited to see if the medication would work.

"You should get some sleep, Doc," he said, finally meeting her gaze. "If I need any more I can handle it." He gestured to the bottle she'd left on the table next to her bag.

"That's all right, Hennessey. You're my patient. I think I'd be more comfortable keeping an eye on you for a while."

Resigned to his fate, he heaved a put-upon sigh and closed his eyes.

Elizabeth glanced at the clock—two-thirty. She should go back to bed, but she doubted she would sleep now. Not after that awful dream and not with Hennessey uncomfortable.

She watched him try to lay still, his hand on his stomach and she wished there was a way to make the medicine work faster, but there wasn't. It would take ten to twenty minutes. She thought about what they'd eaten for dinner and wondered why she wasn't sick. Then again maybe she would be before the night was through.

As if the thought had somehow stirred some part of her that had still been sleeping, her stomach clenched painfully then roiled threateningly.

She recognized the warning immediately and reached for the bottle to down a dose.

"You, too?"

Her gaze met Hennessey's as she twisted the cap back onto the bottle. "Guess so." She grimaced, as much from the yucky taste as from another knot of discomfort.

A light knock on the door and Stark stuck his head inside. "Any chance I could get some of that?"

Before the night was finished all three agents on duty had come in for medication.

At dawn Joe lay on his side watching Elizabeth sleep in the chair not three feet from his bed. She looked more beautiful than any woman had a right to. Her long hair lay against the crisp white of her robe. And those lips, well, they were pretty damned sweet, too. He would give anything right now to taste her. He would lay odds that she tasted hot and fiery, just like her spirit.

Oh, she tempered the fiery side with that cool, calm facade, but he could feel the hellion breathing flames beneath that ultracontrolled exterior.

His gaze traveled over her chest and down to her hips and then to the shapely legs curled beneath her. She worked so hard at everything she allowed herself to do. He wondered if she would work half as hard to be happy.

This was one lady who didn't fully understand the meaning of the word. He'd read what was available on her childhood. Nice family. Moved around a lot since her father had been military, but there didn't appear to be any deep, dark secrets. What had made Elizabeth Cameron so hard on herself? So determined not to fail when it came to helping others?

That was the sole reason, in Joe's estimation, that put her out of the suspect pool. No way would she do anything to endanger another human being. She simply wasn't wired that way. No amount of money—if money were even an issue for her—would entice her. He understood that completely.

Maddox was dead and Calder and Allen were directors. Joe had been filled in when he was selected for the assignment. Who else could have accessed those files?

Three months ago when he'd had to step in long enough to save this pretty lady's skin, someone had broken into her clinic. Had that been the beginning? Were the files the target then? Or had the whole exercise been about casting suspicion in a different direction?

There was no way to know. All he'd had was Maddox's urgent request for backup. Maddox claimed he'd stumbled onto a plan to go after the files of Dr. Elizabeth Cameron. Someone had evidently connected her to the CIA. Of course she had no files related to the Agency.

The only thing he did know for a certainty was how terrified she was that night. He'd held her close to him and she'd trembled. She'd had no idea what was happening, nor did she now. He was convinced. In any event, her safety was one of the Agency's top priorities.

The idea that someone might be setting her up had crossed his mind. But there was no proof as of yet. There was no evidence of anything. Only three dead agents. Still, a real player would have known the files wouldn't be in her office.

Every precaution was being taken to keep the rest of those agents safe, but some were in the middle of dicey operations with higher priorities requiring that they remain undercover.

Those were the ones most at risk.

Joe wished like hell there was a way to speed up this process, except there simply wasn't. His fingerprints could be altered with a clear substance that formed to his skin in such a way that no one could tell the difference. But his face, that had been done in the only way possible. Surgically. Until the swelling and redness were gone he had no choice but to stay right here.

Not that it was such a hardship.

He wondered if David Maddox had had the first clue that the chemistry would be so strong between Joe and Elizabeth. Surely he wouldn't have requested Joe to go to her rescue all those months ago if he'd had any idea that might be the case. Then again, he had known Joe's reputation, however exaggerated.

It was true that Joe dated often and rarely the same lady more than twice. But not all those dates resulted in sex. Not that he was complaining about the reputation. He'd always enjoyed the hype.

Until now.

That thought came out of nowhere, but when he analyzed the concept he knew it was true. Something about the way Elizabeth looked at him when she talked about his reputation didn't sit right.

He wanted her to respect him at least to some degree. Funny thing was, he'd never once worried about that before. He studied the woman sleeping so peacefully. Why was it that what she thought about him mattered so much?

His job performance had always been above reproach. He did what he had to do no matter the cost. Not a single doubt had ever crossed his mind on that score. People respected his professional ability, no question. If anyone had ever been suspect of him personally he hadn't noticed.

Maybe that was the issue at hand here. Had the doctor's blatant distaste with his so-called reputation finally made him take a hard look at what someone else thought about him as a man…as a human being?

He closed his eyes and blocked her image from view.

He didn't want to think anymore. His stomach still felt a little queasy and his face hurt.

Why look for more trouble?

Chapter Seven

Just over two weeks after surgery the bandages were gone, but some of the swelling and redness remained. All in all, Elizabeth was quite pleased with Hennessey's progress in that respect.

It was the tension brewing between them that she could have done without.

From the moment the last of the bandages had come off a subtle shift had occurred between them. Quite frankly Elizabeth couldn't say for sure whether it was her or him or if that was actually when it began. But something had changed on a level over which neither of them appeared to have any control.

Or at least she didn't.

Admittedly she couldn't read Hennessey's mind, but she didn't doubt for a second that he suffered some amount of discomfort related to the tension as well.

And to think, she could have been soaking up the sun and drinking martinis the past two weeks.

She blew out a breath and folded the last of her laundry. The Agency had delivered her luggage the day after her arrival, but a number of the outfits she'd packed for her vacation were far from what she would have preferred to wear in Hennessey's presence. The bikinis were definitely off-limits. She'd had no choice but to wear the few, more conservative outfits over and over.

Hennessey stuck with jeans and button-up shirts or T-shirts. He went around barefoot most of the time. For some reason that bothered her considerably more than it should. It wasn't that he had unattractive feet. To the contrary. His feet actually fascinated her. Large and well-formed. Like the rest of him.

She rolled her eyes and pushed aside the stupid, stupid obsession she had with the man.

Watching David's face slowly emerge beyond the swelling and redness only made matters worse. Perhaps that was even the catalyst in all of this. She just couldn't be certain of anything.

The last time she'd gotten too close to Hennessey the yearning to lean into his arms had been almost overwhelming.

Was she losing her mind or what?

Thankfully no other agents had been murdered since Motley and his wife. Elizabeth squeezed her eyes shut to block the image of the face she'd transformed for the very purpose of protecting the man behind it.

Hennessey assured her that the investigation was ongoing but all had surrendered to the idea that whoever was behind these killings couldn't be stopped any way but by infiltrating the group David had once affiliated himself with. Another week at least before that could happen.

The one other agent they had initially tried to send undercover to infiltrate the group several weeks ago had been killed in the first twenty-four hours. Using David's face as safe entry was the only hope of getting anywhere near the truth.

Elizabeth sat down on the edge of the bed. She hadn't let herself think too much about David and the past since that night the whole lot of them—she, Hennessey and their guards—had gotten a mild case of food poisoning. Stomach cramps and a few mad dashes to the bathroom but, thankfully, nothing more disconcerting than that.

For days now she had set her emotions outside the goings-on within these walls. She had separated the bond she had shared with the man, David, from the CIA operative, David. It hadn't been that difficult, to her utter surprise. She'd turned off her personal emotions and looked at this operation as a case.

But would there be repercussions later? She was a trained physician. She understood that the human psyche could only fool itself to a certain point before reality would override fantasy.

She had far too many scheduled patients depending upon her for her to take a chance on suffering a psychotic break of any sort. Not that she felt on the verge of any kind of break, but she recognized that things with her weren't as they should be.

Scarcely a week from now her part in this would be over. Surely she could manage another five or six days. She and Hennessey had learned to be cordial to each other most of the time, had even shared a laugh or two.

But then there was the tension. She'd pretty much determined that the source of the steadily increasing tension was sexual. He was a man, she was a woman; plain, old chemistry saw to the rest.

Though she didn't dare guess how long it had been since Hennessey had had sex, she knew exactly how long it had been for her. Four long months. And that last time with David had felt off somehow. As if they were out of sync, no longer in tune to one another.

Elizabeth pushed the memories aside. Those painful recollections had nothing to do with any of this.

She was a woman. She had fundamental needs that had been ignored. End of subject.

When she'd put the rest of her laundry away she went in search of her pupil. Might as well get on with today's lesson. More syntax and inflection. He wasn't that far off. She'd heard him in his room at night practicing with tapes of David's voice. She hadn't asked where the tapes had come from. Interviews from old CIA cases or maybe from surveillance tapes.

As she descended the stairs she wondered if he would let her listen to the tapes. Probably not, since they likely involved cases that she didn't have clearance for. Oh well, why torture herself anyway. David was gone. Listening to old tapes of his voice would be detrimental to her mental health. It didn't take a psychologist to see that one coming around the corner.

At the last step she froze. Hennessey, his back to her, had walked across the room, from the coffee-maker on the counter to the sofa in the middle of the living space. The way he'd moved had stolen her breath. Not like Hennessey at all. Like David.

Exactly like David.

She watched him sit down and take a long swill from his mug. Her hands started to tremble. When had he learned to do that? Their lessons had progressed well but nothing on this level.

Summoning her wits she took the last step

down. "Coffee smells great." Somehow she dredged up a smile.

He did the same, but it looked nothing like a David smile.

Thank God.

Wait. The goal was for him to look, act and speak like David.

"You need to work on that smile," she said as she moved toward the kitchen and the coffee. Maybe a strong, hot cup would help clear her head. Obviously she was a little off this morning.

"That smile was for you, not for the mission," he explained.

She poured herself a cup of steaming brew and decided that, as usual, honesty was the best policy. "I saw you walk across the room. It was uncanny." She turned to face him, the hot cup cradled in her hands. "How did you get so good between yesterday and today?"

Strangely, he looked away before answering. "I did a lot of practicing last night. I didn't want you to be disappointed again today."

That felt like a lie even if it sounded sincere.

She padded across the room and took the seat opposite his position on the sofa. Since he never wore shoes she'd decided she wouldn't bother either.

"I'm glad that how I feel matters to you, Agent Hennessey." She sipped her cup as he analyzed her.

Her interrogation had roused his suspicions. Just another reason for her to be suspect.

He set his cup on the table that separated them. "How you feel matters a great deal to me, Doc."

Since she had refused to call him Joe he had reverted to calling her Doc. She didn't like it but when one resolved to play dirty, one couldn't complain.

"Let's get started," she suggested, resting her cup alongside his.

"Let's," he agreed.

Well, wasn't he Mr. Agreeable this morning? Very strange indeed.

JOE RAN THROUGH the steps with Elizabeth until noon brought Agent Dawson and lunch. Whenever Dawson was on duty he dined with them, so Joe had the opportunity to study his teacher.

Every aspect of her cooperation in this mission felt genuine. Even after more than two weeks in close quarters, he would swear that she was above reproach. But he had to be absolutely certain. Two days before this aspect of the mission began Director Allen had informed him of another part of his assignment: make sure Dr. Cameron hadn't been a party to Maddox's act of treason.

To say Joe had been stunned would be putting it mildly, but like any other assignment, he did his duty.

Director Calder had told her the truth about why she was needed for his operation…at least to a degree. That part Joe had known. He had also already known how to walk and talk like Maddox. He only needed a little extra help with a few of his more intimate mannerisms. More important he needed to know as many details as possible about the relationship they had shared.

Joe had hoped to go about this in a way that wouldn't cause Elizabeth further hurt, but that might prove impossible for two reasons.

Director Allen, Joe's immediate boss, still wasn't convinced of Elizabeth's innocence—despite Joe's assessment. Joe had learned that Director Calder, Allen's boss and *the* director of the CIA, was the only reason stronger measures hadn't been taken to determine her involvement, if any, with what David Maddox had done.

Maddox had sold out his country in several ways, but there was no absolute proof that he was the one who'd released the names. All indications pointed to him, but there were also a number, Allen had suggested, that pointed to Elizabeth as having been in on it with him.

With Maddox dead there was really no way to be certain.

Unless Joe could fool Maddox's primary contact from his final operation.

The only glitch was the fact that the contact was female.

Joe settled his gaze on Elizabeth Cameron and wondered if she'd had any idea that Maddox had maintained an ongoing relationship with another woman.

If she did, she hid it well.

Nothing about her demeanor over the past two weeks and some days had given him the first hint of deceit.

But she was suspicious.

She'd made no secret of it. Just another indicator that she wasn't one to hide her feelings.

"Aren't you hungry, Agent Hennessey?" she asked, drawing his attention back to the table.

Dawson's scrutiny was now on him as well. He wasn't happy with the situation at all. The more Allen pushed for information on Elizabeth, the more dissatisfied Dawson grew. Joe regarded the other man a moment and would have bet his life that the guy had a little crush on the good doctor. Of course Dawson was married with two kids and as faithful as they came in this business.

Joe pushed his plate aside. "I'm good. Let me know when you're ready to get started again."

It wasn't like he could take a walk, but he could go to his room for a few minutes before the next session of alone time with her.

He closed the door to his room and walked over to the dresser. He stared at his face, the one that looked nothing like him and more and more like David Maddox.

In a few days the swelling and redness would be all but gone. Then he could move to the next step.

His colored contacts had already been delivered. Probably by tomorrow he would need to start getting accustomed to wearing them. He doubted it would be a problem. He'd done that part before. It was the drastic change in his face that gave him pause.

He'd been mimicking Maddox's speech and movements for weeks before this. But—he reached up and touched his face—this was different.

The counseling hadn't fully prepared him. He'd thought he would be fine with it, but the more Maddox's face emerged the less prepared he felt.

Nothing had ever affected him this way.

That the worst was likely yet to come didn't help.

He had to find a way to prod intimate details from Elizabeth. How Maddox kissed…how he made love to her was essential to Joe's success. He couldn't go into this without being fully prepared on every level.

The only question that remained at this point was how he would get the answers he needed without hurting Elizabeth with the ugly details.

A knock at his door told him his time for soul searching was up.

"Yeah?"

The door opened and Elizabeth strolled into his room. "I need to understand what's going on here, Hennessey," she demanded. "I get the feeling you've been hiding something from me."

Well, here was his opportunity.

Question was, did he have the guts to take advantage of it?

Only one way to find out.

"Here's the thing." He moved toward her, locked his gaze with hers and let her feel the intensity. He needed her off balance. "One of the contacts Maddox had is female. I can't be certain how close they were, considering his relationship with this group preceded the two of you." That part was a flat-out lie but he was improvising here in an attempt to save her the heartache.

A frown furrowed a path across her brow. "How is that possible? He worked as my handler for a year prior to our…relationship. I thought the operation came later, after he'd gone back into field duty."

This is where things got slippery.

"One of the contacts in his last operation was someone he had known for years." He shrugged as if it was no big deal. "An on-again, off-again flame who unknowingly provided him with useful intelligence from time to time. She's my only safe way into this."

Elizabeth wasn't convinced. Far from it.

"Why haven't you mentioned this before?" The frown had given way to something along the lines of outright accusation. "No one has mentioned anything about a woman."

"You know the drill, Doc," he said, careful to keep the regret from his tone, "need to know. The golden rule we live by every day. You had no compelling need to know this part until now."

"If your superiors told you that excuse would make me feel better about this new information, they were wrong," she said in a calm voice but the turmoil of emotions in her eyes belied her unyielding statement.

"We can move back downstairs to have this conversation," he suggested in deference to her comfort. He felt reasonably certain she didn't want to talk about certain details in the room where he slept.

Her expression hardened—the change was painful to watch. "Don't be ridiculous, Hennessey. I'm a doctor. Nothing you say or ask about the human body or the act of procreation will make me uncomfortable in any setting."

With that point driven straight through his chest like a knife she strode over to his bed and plopped down on the end. "What do you want to know?"

The grim line of her mouth and the cool distance in her eyes telegraphed all he needed to know.

Too late not to hurt her. He'd already done just that.

Regret trickled through him, but there was nothing to do but pursue the subject. He needed the information and the damage was done. Holding back now wouldn't accomplish a damned thing.

"We can start with pet names." He shrugged. "Did he usually call you anything other than Elizabeth?"

"What does this have to do with the other woman?"

"Maybe nothing. But I need to be—"

"Yeah, yeah," she cut in. "I get it."

A moment passed as she appeared to collect her thoughts. She stared at some point beyond him. The drapes on the windows were closed, so certainly not at any enticing view.

"Baby," she said abruptly as her eyes met his once more. "He called me *baby* whenever we…" She cleared her throat. "Whenever we were intimate."

"Baby," he murmured, committing the term to memory.

"No." She shook her head. "Not like that. *Baaaby*. With the emphasis on the first syllable."

"Baaaby," he echoed, drawing out the first syllable as if it were two.

She nodded once. "Yes. Like that."

He propped against the dresser and let her talk. She seemed to know what he needed to ask and he appreciated that more than she could possibly comprehend. She shared the sexual vocabulary Maddox used. His euphemisms for body parts and the words that he whispered in her ear as they made love. With every word, every nuance of her voice he felt closer to her…felt the need to touch her. Tension vibrated through him to the point that every nerve ending felt taut with anticipation of what she would say next.

"He liked for me to be on top," she said, careful to avert her eyes. "When I wasn't on top he was usually…" She cleared her throat. "He liked to get behind me." She fisted her fingers and hugged her arms around her middle. "He was very aggressive. Preferred to be in control other than the being on top thing."

Joe wanted to make her stop, but he couldn't. And yet with each new detail she revealed, his body grew harder, he wanted her more.

"Was there a certain…way he touched you?" he ventured, his throat so tight he barely managed to speak.

She blinked, looked away again. "My…ah…

breasts. He always touched me that way a lot. Even when we were just kissing." She rubbed at her forehead, then quickly clasped her arm back around her.

He couldn't take any more of this. He'd hurt her and tortured himself physically. No more.

"Thank you for sharing such intimate—"

"Don't you want to know how he kissed me?" She glared up at him then, the breath rushing in and out of her lungs. All semblance of calm or submissiveness were gone.

Joe straightened away from the dresser. "We can talk about this some more later. There's—"

She rocketed to her feet. "He wasn't that great when it came to kissing."

Her eyes looked huge in her pale face. He couldn't tell if what he saw there was fear or humiliation. Maybe both, and it tore at his guts.

"He used his tongue too much." She paced the length of the room, then turned and moved back in his direction. "But I got used to it eventually." She shrugged her shoulders, the movement stilted. "I was so busy with my work I didn't have time to be too picky about my sex life. Really, what's a busy woman like me supposed to do?"

Her lips trembled with the last and he had to touch her. She was close enough.

"Elizabeth, I'm sorry. I—"

She drew her shoulder away from his seeking hand but didn't back off. "Are you really?" The accusation in her eyes dealt him another gut-wrenching blow. She took a step closer. "If you're so sorry then what prompted your considerable erection, Agent Hennessey?" She reached out and smoothed a hand over the front of his jeans, molded her palm to his aching hard-on.

He moved her hand away but didn't let go of her arm. "Don't do this to yourself, Elizabeth. I explained to you that the female contact was someone he knew before you came into his life."

"And I know a lie when I hear one, *Joe*."

He closed his eyes and exhaled a weary breath. Maybe he should have been up-front with her sooner. He should never have listened to Director Allen. Elizabeth Cameron was far too smart for these kinds of tactics.

"I had known something was wrong for a while," she said, her voice soft, the fierce attitude having surrendered to the hurt. "We hadn't made love in two months when he died. I'd only seen him two or three times. He called, but never talked for long. I guess I knew it was over. I just didn't know why."

It took every ounce of strength Joe possessed not to tell her the truth about David Maddox. He'd used her. He'd cheated on her all along. The latter came with the territory. No man who hoped to keep a clean relationship with a woman stayed in field operations. It simply wasn't feasible.

"You don't know that," he argued, hoping to salvage her feelings to whatever extent possible. "There could have been a lot of things going on that prevented him from coming to you. Your safety for one thing," he offered, grasping at straws. "Remember he sent me in to rescue you that one night when he was too far away to do it himself."

She nodded distractedly as if her heart was working overtime to justify what her brain wanted to reject.

"I would certainly have taken precautions to protect you if I had been in his shoes. Think about it, Doc. He cared about you. You were and still are a valuable asset to the Agency."

Her eyes met his then and something passed between them, a sense of understanding.

"I'm certain you would have, Hennessey." She inhaled a big breath and then let it out slowly. "But you see I've been lying to myself for a while now." She offered a halfhearted shrug. "I guess it made me feel less gullible."

Joe tightened his hold on her forearm, but carefully avoided pulling her closer as he would very much have liked to do. "Sometimes we believe what we want to believe, Doc, even when we know better."

She searched his eyes for so long, he shifted in hopes of breaking the contact. Didn't work.

"Are you really any different from him, Agent Hennessey?"

He wasn't sure how to answer the question.

"I mean," she frowned in concentration, "if having sex with a contact would garner you the information you needed, would you go that far?"

When she put it that way, it sounded like the worst kind of sin. "I wish I could say no, but I'd be lying."

An "I see" look claimed her expression. "Well, at least you're honest."

"I won't lie," he told her in hopes of making the point crystal clear, "unless there is no other way, Doc. Lying is not something I enjoy, but it's part of my job more often than not."

She stared up at him then, puzzled. "Did you know I would give you the information you needed without your having to seduce me?"

"Doc, this situation isn't the same. You came into this knowing the mission."

Her gaze narrowed ever so slightly. "Did I really?"

He had to smile. "To the extent you needed to know, yes."

"But you didn't answer my question," she countered, refusing to give an inch. "Would you have re-sorted to seducing me if necessary?"

"I had my orders, Doc, and seducing you wasn't included." When she would have turned to leave, he caught her wrist once more and drew her back. "Had I not been restrained by my orders, I can't say I wouldn't have tried. But the effort wouldn't have been about the mission."

She searched his eyes again…as if looking for an-swers to questions she couldn't voice. He wanted to lean down and brush his lips across hers. Just for a second, just long enough to feel the softness of hers.

But she walked away before he'd mentally beaten back his deeply ingrained sense of duty and did just that. He closed his eyes and cursed himself for the fool he was. He should have kissed her, should have shown her what a real kiss was like. Not some ego-tistical bastard's sloppy attempts.

He'd had that moment and he'd let it slip away. Part of him had felt certain for just a fleeting instant that she wanted him to kiss her.

"Oh."

He looked up, discovered her waiting at the door as if she'd only just remembered something of ut-most importance and had decided to tell him before she forgot.

"I suppose I should tell you that you might have a bit of a problem with the female contact."

Confusion joined the other tangle of thoughts in his head. "What kind of problem?"

"I believe I would avoid making love to her if at all possible, otherwise I'm certain she will recognize you as an imposter."

His delayed defensive mechanism slammed into place. What the hell was she trying to say? "You noticed a difference between Maddox and me?" he challenged. He knew where this was headed. She'd gotten a good feel of him fully aroused. He wondered if she would actually have the guts to cut him off at the knees, which was, in her opinion, what he imagined he deserved.

She nodded somberly. "I'm afraid so, Agent Hennessey. David was considerably—"

He held up both hands, cutting her off. "I don't think I want to hear this." And here he'd been feeling sorry as hell for her.

"I was just going to say," she went on as she planted one hand firmly on her hip, "that David was way, way *smaller* than you and I doubt any woman still breathing would fail to notice."

Chapter Eight

Elizabeth lay in bed that night and considered what Hennessey had told her. Her initial response had been to deny all of it. But she had known he was telling the truth. If she'd had the first reservation, his genuine regret would have allayed any and all.

Joe hadn't lied to her. He'd tried to protect her.

She closed her eyes and remembered the way he'd looked at her as she'd given him the details of her intimacies with David. That the connection had made her restless to the point of becoming moist in places she'd thought on permanent vacation startled her. Just watching him react to her words had set her on the verge of sexual release.

No man had ever managed that…not for her.

All this time she'd considered herself somewhat lacking in the libido department, but Hennessey made her feel alive and on fire. How could that be?

From a purely psychological standpoint she understood that she had been celibate for longer than usual and she was still hurting from those final months before David had died. She'd known something wasn't right. Now she knew what.

There had been another woman.

Maybe his involvement with her had been purely business, but that didn't make her feel any better. Then again, Hennessey could be correct in his suggestion that David had been trying to protect her. But that would be giving him far too much of a benefit of the doubt. Even she wasn't that gullible.

She and David had been over at least two months before his death.

So why had he kept coming back? Why those final calls? Why hadn't he just told her it was over? It wasn't like he had made any sort of major commitment.

Like any other woman, she had considered he might be the one. That the two of them could perhaps move to the next stage. Get married and start a family. But deep down, especially those last few months, she had known it was going to end.

She banged her fist against the mattress. Why on God's green earth would she get involved with another man like David Maddox?

Evidently she was just as gullible as she'd thought. And seriously out of touch with her education level.

For goodness sakes, plain old common sense screamed at the utter stupidity of this move.

And still she couldn't help how she felt.

Yes, Hennessey was CIA just like David had been.

Yes, he was handsome and charming and sexy.

Just like David.

But there was one significant difference.

She thought of the way she'd touched him. Couldn't imagine how she'd ever worked up the nerve to make that bold move. She hadn't actually. She'd acted on instinct. Without thought.

Her heart bumped into a faster rhythm even now at the memory. There was no comparison between the two when it came to matters below the belt. Joe Hennessey was far more well endowed than David. No way would a former lover *not* notice that disparity.

Elizabeth flopped onto her side and pushed away the confusing thoughts. She refused to get involved with another man until she knew all the facts related to her last relationship.

Was it possible that David had used her for more than mere sex?

She chewed her bottom lip and let the concept penetrate fully. Didn't banish it immediately as she did when she was first asked to be a part of this. David knew the identities of the agents she'd transformed the same as she did. At least he had until the last year. They hadn't discussed the last three she'd done because there had been no reason. He was no longer her handler and like any good member of CIA personnel, she hadn't told.

Nor had he asked.

If he'd wanted to know, why didn't he bring up the subject? Never, not once did he ever, ever ask any questions. He hadn't even appeared interested.

But was that a front to keep her fooled?

She sat up, slung off the covers.

The conspiracy theories were rampant now.

She'd never get any sleep at this rate.

Could he, if he were guilty of this heinous betrayal, have listened in on her conversations with Agent Dawson?

Impossible. Dawson always picked her up and took her to a secure location before giving her any details.

They never talked in her car, on her phone, landline or cell, or at her house.

It simply wasn't done.

And David would have known those hard and fast rules far better than her.

A cold, rigid knot of panic fisted in her stomach.

He would also know how to bug her clothing, her purse, her body for that matter, in such a way that no one could tell.

"Oh, God."

Wait. Maybe she'd seen one too many spy movies. The whole idea was ridiculous.

But people were dead…more might die.

She had to know for sure.

The only way to do that was to go home and look for herself. She would never voice those thoughts about David without some sort of confirmation. It just wouldn't be fair. She had loved him. She couldn't betray him like that simply because Joe Hennessey planted the seed in her mind.

Yes, things had been wrong somehow between her and David those last few months but did that mean he had done anything wrong? She didn't know. One thing was certain, Hennessey had said there were only a handful of people who knew the names of those agents who were being picked off one by one.

David Maddox had been one of them.

Not giving herself time to change her mind, she slipped on her clothes and shoes, grabbed her purse and headed for her door.

Holding her breath she opened it.

The hall was clear.

After taking a moment to gather her courage she eased out into the hall and moved soundlessly to the stairs.

Ten seconds later she was in the laundry room at the rear exit.

Now for the real test.

The house was watched twenty-four/seven.

There was really no way to leave without being caught.

That left only one option.

She dug her cell phone from her purse and called the one person she knew without doubt she could trust.

"HENNESSEY WON'T be happy about this." Her driver wagged his head side to side resignedly.

"Just get me into my house, Agent Dawson," she urged. "If anyone learns we sneaked out I'll take full responsibility."

Dawson exhaled loudly. "I don't think that'll keep me out of trouble, Dr. Cameron, and it definitely isn't necessary. When it comes to your safety I'm the one who is responsible."

"I'm sorry, Agent Dawson," she relented. He was right. "I don't know what I was thinking. I don't want to get you into any trouble."

He didn't slow to turn around. He just kept driving through the darkness toward Georgetown proper and her brownstone.

"It's all right, Dr. Cameron." He glanced at her, let her see his determination in the dim glow from the dash lights. "If it means this much to you, then I'm more than willing to take the risk."

Why were all the good ones taken?

Elizabeth sank back into her seat.

Just her luck.

The image of Joe Hennessey zoomed through her thoughts and she immediately exorcised him. Whether or not he was one of the good guys was yet to be seen. Just because he made her pulse leap and her heart stumble didn't mean he was right for her. All it meant was that she needed to recoup some semblance of a healthy sex life. As Hennessey would no doubt say, she needed to get laid. Come to think of it, he would probably be happy to oblige her if she were to suddenly turn stupid again.

And she had zero intention of doing that.

As they neared Elizabeth's home, Agent Dawson said, "We'll park on the street behind your house and enter from the rear if that'll work for you."

She nodded, then remembered he probably wasn't looking at her. "That'll definitely work."

"Once we get out," he went on, "we need to move quickly."

"I understand." Her heart started to beat a little faster at the idea that she might very well be in danger. She'd told herself that being exiled to the safe house was about protecting Hennessey's transformation, but maybe that wasn't all there was to it.

She shivered. Maybe that's what Dawson was worried about more so than getting into trouble.

Surely he would tell her if that was the case.

Something else she didn't need to worry about.

The street was still and dark save for a few streetlamps posted too far apart. Agent Dawson parked his sedan behind another lining the sidewalk and they got out.

"Stay behind me," he instructed.

Elizabeth did as he asked, following right behind him as they moved through the side yard of the house directly behind hers. On this street the homes were small, single bungalows with postage-stamp-sized yards. A tall wooden fence lined the rear boundaries, separating these private yards from the shared space behind the brownstones. She and Agent Dawson stayed outside the fenced area, wading through the damp grass.

Her home, like the ones on either side of it, was dark, but the area around the back door was lit well enough by moonlight that she could unlock the door without the aid of a flashlight.

"Let me check it out first."

She stood just inside her kitchen while he checked out the rest of the house. When he'd returned and given her the go-ahead she took his flashlight, his assertion not to turn on any lights in the house unless absolutely necessary ringing in her ears, and went straight to her room while he guarded the rear entrance.

Though she and Agent Dawson had taken a number of journeys together in the past year, this was her first ever covert adventure with the man. She was quite impressed with his stealth and finesse.

He hadn't dragged her into an alley and held her clamped against his body as Agent Hennessey had, but admittedly, the circumstances were different so there could be no actual comparison.

"Focus, Elizabeth," she ordered, putting aside thoughts of Hennessey and his muscular body.

If David had wanted to learn about her work for the CIA he would have had to "bug" her. She felt confident that the CIA regularly monitored the vehicles they used and, certainly, Agent Dawson would keep himself bug free. But she, on the other hand, had no idea about such things. Hadn't even anticipated the need.

First she checked through every single undergarment she wore to work. Nothing. She ran the beam of light over her room and located the jewelry box. Jewelry really wasn't something she cared to accessorize with but occasionally she did wear a necklace or bracelet.

Nothing unexpected there.

That left only her clothes and her purses.

She did regularly change bags.

And each time Agent Dawson picked her up she had already changed into her street clothes. She wasn't like a lot of the medical professionals who lurked around in public while wearing scrubs. Not that it was such a bad thing, she supposed. She simply wasn't comfortable doing so.

She pulled the door to her walk-in closet almost completely shut, leaving just enough room to reach out with one hand and flip on the switch. Once the door was closed, she set Agent Dawson's flashlight aside and started her search.

Every jacket, skirt and pair of slacks had to be examined from top to bottom, inside and out. She didn't know that much about electronic listening or surveillance devices but, again, plain old common sense told her they could come in virtually any shape or form.

Before diving into her clothes, she went through her bags. There were fewer and they were certainly easier to rummage around in.

Nothing suspicious. A few crumbs from the packs of snack crackers she carried in one. A couple of dollars in another. Wow! A peppermint breath mint from her favorite restaurant in the last one she picked up.

She unwrapped the mint and popped it into her mouth before moving onto her clothes.

This would take forever.

If Hennessey woke up she would be in serious trouble. She wondered if Dawson had told the other agent on duty about their little excursion. He hadn't mentioned it and she hadn't asked.

Hurry! Hurry!

Her hand stilled, backed up and moved over the pocket of her favorite slacks. A tiny bump. Her heart thundering, she reached inside and withdrew a small wad of chewed gum wrapped in tissue.

"Great," she huffed.

The door to her closet suddenly opened and Elizabeth wheeled around to identify her unexpected guest.

Not Dawson.

For several moments she couldn't breathe.

David.

Then the lingering redness and swelling crashed into her brain.

Hennessey.

"We've already done this, Doc," he said calmly but those startling blue eyes gave away the fury brewing behind that laid-back exterior. "Our technicians didn't find anything. You're not likely to either."

"This wasn't Agent Dawson's idea," she said quickly. "I forced him to bring me here." She smoothed her suddenly sweaty palms over her thighs. "I threatened to come alone if he didn't bring me."

"Dawson and I have already spoken."

"Oh." She looked around at the wreck she'd made of her closet. And she'd thought the worst thing she had to worry about was falling prey to Hennessey's charm. Look at what she'd done. She wasn't equipped to play this kind of game. "I guess I'll just clean up this mess." She manufactured a shaky smile for him. She refused to admit that coming here had been too dumb for words. She'd needed to come. "You don't have to hang around. Dawson will bring me back."

"I sent Dawson back already."

She blinked, tried to hide her surprise. "Okay." She reached for a jacket lying in a twist on the floor. "I'll be quick."

"I'll be waiting."

He exited the closet, closing the door behind him.

Elizabeth stood there for a time, grappling for composure.

David had cheated on her. She didn't need any evidence. She *knew*.

The CIA obviously thought he'd used her as well or they wouldn't have been nosing around in her house. There was no arguing that conclusion. A part of her wanted to be angry, wanted to scream, but what was the point? It was done. David had done this to her.

Elizabeth closed her eyes and fought back the tears. She would not cry for or about him. He was gone. He'd been gone for a long time before he died.

Any other emotional wringers she put herself through related to him were a total waste of energy.

Slowly, piece by piece, she put the contents of her closet back to order, purses and all.

She thought about snagging a few items to take back with her, but she wouldn't be there much longer. There was no need.

As soon as she opened the door she flipped off the closet light. It took several moments for her eyes to adjust to the darkness. She thought about turning on the flashlight but there was really no reason since she knew her way around her own bedroom.

"You finished with what you came here to do?"

She stumbled back, gasped, before her eyes finally made out the image of someone sitting on the bench at the foot of her bed. The voice left no question as to identity.

Hennessey.

"Yes, I guess so."

Since he made no move to get up she sat down next to him.

Joe told himself to get up, to get the hell out of her bedroom, but he couldn't.

He kept torturing himself over and over with the images her words evoked even now. He knew with certainty that Maddox had made love to her in this room. With her on top…with him behind her. His hands on her breasts.

Every breath he drew into his lungs carried the scent of her. Her room, her whole house, smelled of her. Nothing but her. She was a doctor. She was never home long enough to cook. Only to soak in a tub of fragrant water. To shower with her favorite soap and shampoo.

She didn't wear perfume. Only the soap or maybe the subtle essence of the lotion sitting on her bedside table. He hadn't needed to turn on a light since arriving to see any of this. He'd been here with the techs when they'd gone through her things. He'd touched the undergarments she wore next to her skin. Had inhaled the scent of her shampoo.

And then he'd watched her. Twenty-four/seven for weeks. Until he'd thought of nothing but her.

"He used me, didn't he?"

The fragile sound of her voice carried more impact than if she'd screamed at him from the top of her lungs.

"Yes, we believe so."

Silence.

"For how long?"

"That we don't know."

"That's why you said you wouldn't lie—" she swallowed "—like he did."

"Yes."

"So…" She sucked in a ragged breath, tearing the oxygen out of his with the vulnerable noise. "Maybe it was real in the beginning?"

"Maybe."

More silence.

"I loved him, you know."

He squeezed his eyes shut against the tears he heard in her voice. "I know."

"Do you know how he died?"

That information was off-limits to her…but how could he let her wonder. "He died in the line of duty. That's all I can tell you."

"Will you take me back now?"

"Yes."

Joe stood. He reached for her hand and led her from her room, along the short hall and down the narrow staircase. He'd been in her home enough times to know the layout probably as well as she did.

He locked the door for her when they'd exited the rear of the house. Then they walked quietly through the moonlight until they reached his sedan.

Nothing else was said as they made the trip back to the safe house.

Joe took several zigzagging routes to ensure they weren't followed.

Daylight wasn't far off when they finally parked in the garage.

She got out and went inside. He didn't follow immediately.

He needed to walk off some of the tension shaking his insides. He'd alternated between wanting to yell at her and wanting to kiss her. Managing to get by without doing either was a credit to his sheer willpower.

He'd wanted to make her forget that bastard Maddox, but he'd resisted.

She didn't need him taking advantage of her vulnerability.

He might be a lot of things, but that kind of jerk he wasn't.

Inside the house he trudged up the stairs. He dreaded lying down again knowing sleep would not come. Their earlier candid discussion had kept him awake the greater portion of the night as it was.

He'd known when she left the house.

He'd followed but hadn't interfered at first, only when she'd stayed too long he'd had no choice.

The time he'd given her had been enough. She'd come to her own conclusions in her own time which was best. Anything he'd said or asserted would only have been taken with a grain of salt, would have put her on the defensive.

He didn't bother with the light in his room. Just kicked off his shoes and peeled off his shirt, inhaling one last time the smell of her where her arm had brushed against him as they'd sat on the bench in her room.

He stripped off his jeans and climbed into the bed. He was tired. Maybe he'd catch a few winks after all.

The instant his eyes closed her voice whispered through his head. Every intimate detail she'd relayed today echoed through his weary mind. He fisted his fingers in the sheet, tried his best not to think about how her nipples would feel against the palms of his hands. He licked his lips and yearned for her taste.

He could have gotten up and taken a cold shower. Probably should have. Instead he lay there and allowed the sensuous torture to engulf him. Didn't resist.

He was too far gone for that.

ELIZABETH LAY in her bed, her knees curled up to her chest. Director Calder had known the truth. Hennessey had known. Maybe even Dawson.

She was the only one who hadn't had any idea that David was using her.

How could she have been so blind?

She clenched her jaw to hold back the fury. How could he do that to her? He'd professed his love for her and all along he'd been using her.

How long had he planned his little coup?

At least one thing was for sure, he hadn't gotten to enjoy the fruits of his evil deeds.

A part of her felt guilty for thinking about his death that way, but the more logical part of her reveled in it. He might have used her, but he'd paid the ultimate price in the end. Along with three of the agents she'd given new faces.

Her stomach roiled with dread.

Who else would die before Hennessey could stop this?

Was there nothing she could do?

Give them new faces?

But if it were that easy the CIA would have suggested it.

No.

It would never be that simple.

Hennessey would have to risk his life to get close enough to the devils behind this to take them out.

One was a woman.

A woman who would undoubtedly expect him to make love to her as David likely had. And then she would know that Hennessey was an imposter.

Heat rushed through Elizabeth in spite of her troubling thoughts. She just couldn't help the reaction. She needed him—wanted him.

But that would be yet another monumental mistake on her part. She didn't need to make any more mistakes far more than she needed to indulge in heart-pounding sex with Hennessey.

But she could dream about him. And how it would feel to have him kiss her and hold her close.

There was no rule against fantasies.

She remembered that night three months ago when he'd held her against him in the darkness. His body had felt strong, powerful. His muscles hard from years of disciplined physical activity and maybe from the feel of her backside rubbing against him.

When she'd touched him tonight…felt the size of him against her palm, she'd wanted to rip off his clothes and look at all of him for a very long time. Just look. Then she wanted to learn all there was to know about him on a physical level.

How he tasted…how his hands would feel gliding over her skin…

She drifted off to sleep with that thought hovering so close she could have sworn it was real.

Chapter Nine

Director Calder remained seated at the table but Joe was far too restless to stay in one place. He poured himself a fourth cup of coffee and grimaced at the bitter taste.

"You're absolutely certain you're ready to do this?" Calder asked once more. "Any further delay could be detrimental to our chances, but I'm not willing to run the risk of sending you in too soon."

"Do I look ready?"

Joe faced the man the president himself had chosen to oversee one of the nation's most important security agencies and let him look long and hard. He'd put the colored contacts in this morning. He'd wanted to try them out while Elizabeth was preoccupied going over dates with Dawson.

Calder moved his head slowly from side to side. "You look just like him." He blew out a breath. "It's uncanny, Hennessey."

Joe nodded. "I know." Even he had been shaken this morning. As he'd gone about the morning ritual of going to the john, he'd caught a glimpse of his reflection in the mirror and done a double take. His tousled hair had looked like it always did first thing in the morning, but his face…well, suffice to say it wasn't his.

The swelling and redness was gone entirely—at least as far as he could tell. It was as if he'd gone to bed last night with a little of both and then this morning *poof.*

He'd gone back to his room and called Dawson. He needed a distraction for Elizabeth until he could get used to the change himself.

She'd mentioned a day or so ago that sometimes this sort of abrupt change happened, but he wasn't prepared. He seriously doubted that she would be either.

Once he'd put the contacts in he'd had to brace himself on the counter to keep from staggering back from the mirror. The transformation had been incredible.

He, for all intents and purposes, was David Maddox.

"We knew Elizabeth was good," Calder went on, "but this is beyond our greatest expectations."

Joe had been watching this new face emerge from the aftermath of surgery and he'd known the transformation would get him by, but this was far more than that. This was almost scary.

He thought about Elizabeth and the way she'd sneaked back to her home the other night. He'd wanted to comfort her. To hold her until she came to terms with the way Maddox had used her. But he'd held back. She hadn't needed any more confusion. She'd needed someone who understood…someone to listen and he'd done both those things.

In the three days since she'd been distant. Not that he could blame her. She'd just learned that the man she'd loved had cheated on her, used her. Had likely never really cared about her. That was a hard pill to swallow, even for a fiercely intelligent woman who was also a skilled surgeon.

Learning the truth had, in a way, facilitated what had to be done. Elizabeth had focused more intently on their work and so had he. A lot had been accomplished.

He was ready for this mission.

"Where is she now?"

"She's with Dawson. He's going over significant dates with her to see if she recalls anything relevant."

Calder frowned. "Haven't we already done that?"

"I needed her distracted for this meeting." Joe leaned against the counter and forced down more of the coffee.

"You're still convinced she had nothing to do with this," Calder wanted to know.

"Totally convinced." Joe set his cup in the sink. He'd had all of that brew he could stomach. He moved to the table. Though he still felt too restless he needed Calder to see just how convinced he was. "She had no idea what Maddox was up to. I think you know that."

Calder nodded. "I do. It's Allen who's still not on the same page with us. But I'll take care of him."

Joe breathed easy for the first time since this operation started. He knew what Maddox had done. No way would he stand idly by and let Elizabeth take the fall for anything that bastard did.

"Is it essential that we wait the next three days before I go in?" Joe ventured. He knew the plan as well as anyone, but he wasn't sure staying here with Elizabeth for seventy-two more hours was a good idea.

"We have to trust our intelligence, Hennessey," Calder said, telling him what he already knew but didn't want to hear. "Word is that she'll be in-country in just over forty-eight hours. We don't want to rush this thing."

The director was right, no question. But Joe's instincts kept nagging at him to get into position. There was nothing specific he could put his finger on. The best analysts in the world were processing new intelligence every hour of every day. If anything had changed, Joe would know it right after Calder.

The fact that Calder was literally sitting in on this one personally made it the highest priority mission. So far three agents had been ambushed, two while involved in an ongoing mission. Stopping those assassinations was imperative. Additionally, Dr. Elizabeth Cameron had been Calder's brainchild. He had personally brought her into the Agency's family. He and Dawson, discounting Maddox, were the only ones allowed to approach her, until this operation. Joe had a feeling that Calder felt responsible for the woman's safety as well as her actions, good, bad or indifferent.

When Calder had gone, Joe went back to his room to study his reflection in an attempt to grow accustomed to the face staring back at him. It wasn't easy, considering he would have liked to rip Maddox apart himself if someone hadn't beat him to the punch. That the bastard's body hadn't been recovered only infuriated Joe all the more. But three credible eyewitnesses had testified to what they had seen. The shooter had been found but he'd refused to talk and ended up offing himself the first chance he got.

Whoever had sanctioned Maddox's termination was powerful enough that his reputation alone had ensured the shooter wouldn't turn on him.

The remaining questions were about Maddox's associates. Who had wanted the list of agents with new faces? Even if Joe infiltrated the group, could he be sure they would talk? Not even the CIA could stop a nameless entity. A name, a face, they needed anything to go on.

Before more bodies piled up.

"I'M SORRY, Agent Dawson," Elizabeth said finally. "That's everything I remember. If there was anything else during that time frame I can't recall."

"That's all right, Dr. Cameron." He closed the document on the computer. "What you remembered will be useful." He stood then. "We should probably get back."

Elizabeth followed him from the borrowed office in the rear of the downtown library. She wasn't sure why he had insisted they review all the newspaper reports from the three months prior to David's death. Maybe to prod her memories. She hadn't remembered anything she hadn't told them already. But she hadn't minded taking another shot at it. She was only human. It was just as likely as not that she could have forgotten something relevant.

But she hadn't.

If she were honest with herself she would admit that getting away from the safe house for a few hours was a good thing. Other than her one excursion back to her brownstone she hadn't left in three weeks. She was thankful for the respite.

The other night when she'd had to face the reality of what she'd denied about David for months she'd almost asked Hennessey to sleep with her. She'd so desperately needed someone to cling to, she'd resisted that crushing need by the slimmest of margins. Thank God he'd had his head about him. All he would have had to have done was touch her, in the most innocent fashion, and she would have surrendered without a fight.

For the past three days she had felt pretty much numb. Empty, really. Everything she'd thought to be true about David was nothing but lies. Learning that truth had hurt, but not so much as it would have had she not suspected that there was someone else months before his death.

But just beneath the numbness she had felt these last few days lay something else that simmered steadily. She told herself it was nothing, but that was a lie. She'd been attracted to Hennessey since that first night three months ago when he'd shown up to play bodyguard. That attraction hadn't abated. Not in the least. But with David's death and the idea that agents she had given new faces were dying, she hadn't been able to think about that for any length of time. Even now, maybe it was the exhaustion or just the plain old emptiness still hanging on, her developing feelings for Hennessey were too far from the surface to analyze with any accuracy.

And why in the world would she even want to go there?

Hennessey was the farthest thing from what she needed as a man could get. He represented everything wrong she'd done in her last relationship.

Why couldn't the irrational part of her that wanted to reach out to him see that?

He was one of those dangerous types. A man who risked everything, every single day of his life. She couldn't count on him any more than she had been able to count on David, excluding his various and sundry betrayals.

What she needed was safe, quiet, bookish.

A man who spent his days behind a desk reviewing accounts or reports. Not some gun-toting, cocky hotshot who kicked ass at least twice before lunch most days.

She closed her eyes and tried to clear her mind as Dawson took the necessary clandestine route back to the safe house. Thank God no more agents had died.

And although she hadn't seen Hennessey this morning she knew the time was close at hand for his departure. The swelling and redness had been all but gone yesterday. She'd struggled with focusing on the work rather than the end result.

It was far less painful to look at each feature individually rather than to look at his face as a whole. But the one saving grace was his eyes.

Joe Hennessey had the most amazing blue eyes. Even with his face changed, those startling blue eyes made it virtually impossible to notice anything else.

His flirtatious personality emanated from those eyes.

The deep brown of David's still haunted her dreams occasionally, but lately the only man she'd been dreaming about was Hennessey.

Such an enormous mistake.

Why couldn't she get that through her head?

She saw it coming. If she could just hold out a little while longer.

Three more days and she would go back to her life. He would go wherever it was David's associates were suspected of being and most likely they would never again see each other. The end.

She squeezed back the emotion that attempted to rise behind her eyelids. She'd done her job, had prepared Hennessey for the operation. There was nothing else she could do. Nothing else she should do until this was over. Then she would reverse the procedure, assuming he survived.

Getting on with her life was next on her list. She could not wallow in the past or pine after a man who would do nothing but bring her more heartache.

She had to be smart. Making the right decisions about her future had to be next on her agenda. Her career was everything she'd hoped it would be. Now if she could only say the same about her private life.

There was only one way to make that happen.

Put David Maddox and anything affiliated with him out of her head. Move forward and never look back.

It was simple.

But before she could do that she had to be sure she had passed along every tidbit Joe Hennessey would need to survive the coming mission. Even though she fully understood that a relationship between them would be a mistake, she didn't want him hurt. Whatever she could do to facilitate his efforts was not only necessary but nonnegotiable.

By the time she and Dawson had reached the safe house it had started to rain and a cloak of depression had descended upon her despite her internal pep talk. The sky had darkened, much like her mood.

When the garage door had closed, ensuring no one who might be watching had seen her emerge from the vehicle, she got out and went inside. She shook off the nagging weight that wanted to drag her into a pit of regret and dread. This wasn't the end, she assured herself, this was a new beginning.

Hennessey would move on with what he did best and she would refocus some of her energy into her personal life. She'd neglected that area for far too long.

Life was too short to spend so much time worrying about all the things she'd done wrong. All the mistakes she'd made. She had to look ahead, move forward.

How many times did she give her patients that very advice? All the time. The kind of devastation that wrought physical deformities more often than not was accompanied by chronic clinical depression. At times, even after full recovery, a patient would linger in the throes of depression's sadistic clutches. Patients had to make a firm choice, to wallow in the past or move into the future.

She had to do the same.

No more dwelling on yesterday. Time to move forward.

Elizabeth hesitated at the door, pushed her glasses up the bridge of her nose and took a long, deep breath.

"Your future begins now," she whispered.

Without looking back, Elizabeth pushed through the door and into the laundry room of the safe house.

The smell of Chinese cuisine alerted her to the time. Lunch. Stark must be on duty. Whenever he was the agent in charge of bringing in meals, his food of choice was Chinese. Not that she minded, she liked fried rice, a lot.

Agent Stark looked up as she entered the kitchen section of the large living space. "You're just in time, Dr. Cameron."

She inhaled deeply. "I noticed."

"I see you made it back, Doc."

Elizabeth looked up at the sound of Hennessey's voice. Her chest seized and her eyes widened in disbelief. She closed her eyes and reopened them in an effort to clear her vision. It was still him...*David.*

"I started wearing the contacts," he said as he tapped his right temple. "The change in eye color definitely put the finishing touch on the look."

He said the words so nonchalantly. She blinked again, told herself to breathe. She couldn't. Managing a nod was the best she could do.

Hennessey gestured to the counter. "You hungry?"

He moved like Hennessey. He spoke like Hennessey. But no matter that she told herself that what she saw was an illusion she, herself, helped to create, she just couldn't get past it. Pain twisted in her chest, radiated outward, encompassing her entire being.

"I'll..." She swallowed against the lump in her throat. "I'll have something later."

She rushed past him, couldn't bear to look a moment longer. This felt so wrong...so damned wrong.

Taking the stairs as fast as she dared she made it to her room in record time. She closed the door and slumped against it.

A full minute was required for her to catch her breath, to slow her heart rate. To form a coherent thought.

She should have been prepared for this moment. David's face had emerged a little more each day. She'd watched the features move from discolored and distorted to smooth and glowing with the tint of health.

All those things she'd expected...she'd been prepared for. But this...

It was the eyes she hadn't been fully equipped to see...to look into.

David's eyes.

As dark as a moonless night.

She'd gotten lost in them so many times. Not once had she been able to read his intentions. Whether it was the deep, murky color or just his skill at evasive tactics she couldn't be sure. But the mystery had been part of the attraction. He'd drawn her in so easily.

How in the wide world could she have believed she could do this?

Elizabeth closed her eyes and blocked the tears; forced away the images.

She couldn't do this.

And why should she?

She'd done her part.

There was no reason for her to stay a minute longer.

A light rap on the door behind her made her breath hitch again. She pressed a hand to her chest and reached for some semblance of calm.

She had to get her composure back into place.

All she needed to do was tell Agent Dawson she was ready to go home. Her work here was finished.

No one could argue that infinitely valid point.

Steeling herself against the turmoil of emotions attempting to erupt inside her she straightened away from the door, then turned to answer it.

It would be Hennessey.

It would be tough.

But she was strong.

She smoothed her damp palms over her skirt and pulled in another much needed breath.

Then she opened the door.

David's eyes stared down at her.

Not David, she reminded herself.

Hennessey. Agent Joe Hennessey.

"We should talk about this."

She looked away, let his voice be her buoy. Hennessey's voice. Low, husky, shimmering with mischief just beneath the surface. Not the slow, deep cadence of David. Why was it she'd never realized how very, nearly calculating his voice had been? It wasn't until she'd come here with Hennessey that she'd understood what sexy really was.

David hadn't been sexy...he'd been bawdy.

Elizabeth squared her shoulders and did what she should have done days ago. "Agent Hennessey, clearly I've contributed all to this operation that I have to offer. I'm certain you won't be needing my services any longer. With that in mind, I'm sure you'd understand if I chose not to have this discussion." She braced to close the door. "Please let Agent Dawson know I'll be ready to go in ten minutes."

She had expected him to argue.

She'd even expected him to try to stop her.

But the last thing she'd expected was for him to kiss her.

He took her face in both his hands and pulled her mouth up to meet his.

Just like that.

His lips felt firm but somehow more yielding than she had expected. His mouth was hot…ravenous, as if he was starving and she was dessert. She melted against him, couldn't help herself. The sweet feel of her body conforming to his made her shiver with a need so urgent she moaned with the intensity of it.

Sensations cascaded down from her face, following the path of his hands as he stroked her cheeks with his long fingers then slipped lower to caress her throat.

Her heart beat so hard she couldn't breathe… couldn't think. She just kept kissing him back—kept clinging to his strong body, hoping the moment would never end.

"Elizabeth," he murmured against her lips. "I'm sorry. I…" He kissed her harder….

She tried to pull away…tried to push against his chest. But she couldn't bear the thought of taking her hands away from his chest. Even through the cotton shirt she reveled in the feel of the contours of his chest. She suddenly wanted to touch all of him. To see if the rest of his body was as amazing as his chest and the other part she'd already examined.

His arms went around her and for the first time in months she felt safe in a way that had absolutely nothing to do with professional success or inner strength. She wanted this as a woman…and she didn't want it to end.

But it had to end.

She couldn't do this again.

Her hands flattened against his chest and she pushed away from him, not taking her lips from his until it was impossible to reach him anymore.

He opened his eyes and her heart lurched.

"I have to leave now."

She stumbled back from his reach.

"Elizabeth, I can take out the contacts. We can talk."

She closed her eyes, tried to block the visual stimuli. Told herself to listen to his voice. Joe Hennessey…not David. Not David.

"Please." She forced her eyes open again. "I need to go now. There's nothing more I can do."

He looked away, displaying the profile she'd created. David's profile. The slightly longer and broader nose, the more prominent chin.

She swallowed. Looked away.

"This isn't who I am." He gestured to the face she had sculpted. "You know who I am."

She did. That was true. He was Agent Joe Hennessey of the CIA. A dangerous man…her gaze shifted back to his…with an even more dangerous face.

"I do know who you are." The words were strong but she felt cold and hollow. "And I can't do this with a man like you. Not again. The price is too high."

She turned her back to him in the nick of time. She couldn't let him see the foolish tears.

"I'll let Agent Dawson know you're ready to leave."

She heard him walk away.

Finished.

This was finished. No reason for her to stay…to put herself through this.

All she had to do was go home and forget this assignment…forget the man.

Chapter Ten

Elizabeth reviewed the day's messages, her mind on autopilot. That was the way it had been for most of the day. The only time she'd been able to really think clearly and in the moment was when she'd been with a patient. Thankfully three patients who'd been on standby awaiting appointments had been available to fill her day. So far four work-ins were scheduled for tomorrow and then she'd be back on her regular schedule.

Back to her real life.

Her concentration, such as it was, shattered yet again. Elizabeth tossed the messages onto her desk and leaned back in her chair.

This was her life.

Slowly, her heart sinking just a little more, she surveyed her chic office. Clean lines, no clutter. Diplomas and other accolades matted and framed in exquisite detail draped the smooth linen-colored walls. Short pile carpet in the same pale color padded the floor and served as a backdrop to the sleek wood furnishings. The rest of the clinic's decor was every bit as elegant; the treatment rooms equipped with the same spare-no-expense attitude.

The practice shared by herself and two other specialized physicians dominated the east corner of an upscale Georgetown address. Clientele included patients from all over the country as well as a few from abroad. Business boomed to the point that expansion would surely soon be necessary.

All those years of hard work had paid off for Elizabeth in a big way. Professionally she had everything she desired. Everything she'd dreamed about.

But that was where the dream ended.

She'd deluded herself into believing there could be more. That she could throw herself back into a social life. The chances of that doomed plan seeing fruition were about nil—she recognized that now. The cruise had been a last-ditch effort on her part to wake up her sleeping sex life. Not that she'd had any sort of exciting social life in the past. Admittedly she hadn't. But even dating hadn't crossed her mind since David's death. Absolutely nothing had made her want to venture back into the world of the living and the loving.

Until Joe Hennessey popped back in.

All those forbidden feelings Hennessey had aroused three months ago had suddenly reawakened when he waltzed back into her small world with this assignment.

Elizabeth closed her eyes and let the volatile mixture of heat and desire spread through her. He made her want to embark onto that emotional limb of love again. How could she be so dumb when all those diplomas hanging on the walls proclaimed her intelligence?

A light tap on her closed door dragged her away from the disturbing thoughts and back to the harsh reality that she was once more at square one, alone in her office at the end of the day with no place to go and no one with whom to share her successes or her failures.

She forced her eyes open. "Yes."

The door cracked far enough for Dr. Newman, one of her partners, to poke his head into her office. "You busy?"

Elizabeth tacked a smile into place. "Not at all. Come in, Dr. Newman." As long as she'd known Robert Newman—they'd worked closely for four years—they had never moved beyond the professional formalities. She suddenly wondered why that was. He was a very nice man. Safe, quiet, bookish, all the traits she should look for in a companion. That she admired and respected him was icing on the cake. Just another prime example of her inability to form proper social relationships.

His lab coat still looking pristine after a full day of seeing patients, he shoved his hands into his pockets and strolled up to her desk. "Do you have dinner plans?"

Now that startled her. Was he asking her out to dinner? They'd attended the same work-related social functions numerous times, but never as a couple. She blinked, tried to reason whether or not she'd misunderstood.

Had she somehow telegraphed her misery through the walls? Was this a pity invitation?

He cleared his throat when she remained speechless beyond a polite pause. "I thought you might not have had time to shop since you've gotten back. Your cupboards are probably bare."

Oh, yes, this was definitely a dinner *date* invitation.

Now she knew for sure just how little attention she'd paid to the men around her. If she'd had any question, the hopeful look in her colleague's eyes set her straight.

How could she have missed this? She'd had absolutely no idea.

"You would probably be right," she confessed, well aware that any continued stalling would be seen as not only a rebuff but rude. She reached deep down inside and retrieved a decent smile. "To be honest,

I'm beat. I think I need a vacation to recover from my vacation." It wasn't until that moment that she realized how much her affiliation with the CIA had changed the dynamics of her other professional relationships. How many times had she lied to her colleagues about her whereabouts?

Don't go there. Not tonight.

She pushed up from her chair, glanced around her desk to ensure she hadn't forgotten anything that wouldn't wait before meeting Dr. Newman's gaze once more. Disappointment had replaced the hope. "But I'd love a rain check."

Some of the disappointment disappeared. "Sure."

After a brief exchange of war stories about the day's patients, Dr. Newman said good-night and was on his way.

At that moment Elizabeth realized just how very exhausted she felt. A long, hot bath, a couple glasses of wine and a decent night's sleep, she decided, would be her self-prescribed medicine.

After rounding up her purse she headed for the rear exit. She'd already called Agent Dawson and let him know she was ready to go. When she reached the parking lot he waited only steps from the clinic's rear entrance. He would follow her home and then maintain a vigil outside until around nine o'clock and he would be replaced by Stark.

As she slid behind the wheel of her Lexus she regarded the necessity of this measure once more. She hadn't really felt that the added security was necessary but Director Calder had insisted. She'd finally relented and agreed to one week of surveillance. If he felt that strongly, how could she ignore the possibility that he might be right? After all, ferreting out intelligence and analyzing risks was his business.

The drive to her brownstone was uneventful. Before leaving her car at the curb she couldn't go inside without asking Agent Dawson if he'd prefer to come inside. She'd spent the past three weeks holed up with Joe Hennessey, spending time alone with Dawson would be a breeze.

But Agent Dawson declined her offer.

She'd known he would. Dawson was far too much of a stickler for the rules.

Unlike Hennessey.

Or David.

Wasting her time and energy obsessing over the two men she'd allowed herself to get close to was pointless. Why put herself through the additional grief?

How had it been so easy all these years to move through life without getting her heart snagged? Work had been her focus. Until just over a year ago when David had lured her into a relationship. She'd thought it was time. Why not? Most women her age had already been involved in committed relationships. Why shouldn't she? But it had gone all wrong.

Another thought crept into her mind. Maybe she simply wasn't equipped to deal with failure. Her academic and professional life had succeeded on every level. Perhaps the fear of failure kept her from taking emotional risks.

"No more self-analysis," she muttered.

She unlocked her front door and stepped inside. Left all the questions and uncertainty on the stoop.

Home sweet home.

A long, deep breath filled her lungs with the scents of her private existence. The lingering aroma of the vanilla scented candles she loved…the vague hint of the coffee she'd had this morning.

She dug around in the freezer until she found a microwave dinner that appealed to her. Five minutes and dinner would be served. A bottle of chardonnay she'd bought to celebrate the night before departing on her cruise still sat unopened on her kitchen island. Perfect.

Lapsing back into her usual routine as easily as breathing, she set a place at the table, lit a candle and poured the wine. Just because she ate alone didn't mean she couldn't make it enjoyable.

The chicken breast, steamed vegetables and pasta turned out better than she'd expected. Or maybe she was just hungry. She hadn't realized until then that she'd completely forgotten lunch. She did that quite often. But so did most of her colleagues.

The wine did its work and slowly began to relax her. By the time she'd climbed out of the tub she was definitely ready for bed and well on her way to a serious good night's sleep.

She pulled the nightgown over her head and smiled at the feel of the silk slipping along the length of her body. Practical had always been her middle name, but she did love exquisite lingerie. Panties, bras, gowns. She loved sexy and silky. Vivid colors were her favorites. Her bedtime apparel was way different from her day wear. David had always teased her about it.

Cursing herself, she turned out the light and stamped over to her bed. She had to stop letting him sneak into her thoughts. He was dead. Creating his face on another man had torn open old wounds once more. She needed to allow those wounds to heal. Whatever her future held she needed to get beyond the past.

She pulled the sheet back, but a sound behind her stopped her before she slid onto the cool covers. She wheeled around to peer through the darkness.

"It's just me," a male voice said, the sound of it raking over her skin like a rough caress.

She shivered. "Hennessey?" What was he doing here? Had something happened? She felt her way to the table and reached for the lamp.

"Don't turn on the light."

Elizabeth stilled, her fingers poised on the switch.

"I don't want you to see him. I want you to listen to *me*. Only me."

Her heart started to pound. What on earth was he doing here? Had he relieved Agent Dawson? No, that didn't make sense. This was Dawson's mission….

"I don't understand." She wished her throat wasn't so dry. Every part of her had gone on alert to his presence. Her hands wanted to reach out to him, her fingers yearned to touch him. She would not listen to the rest of the whispers of need strumming through her, urging her to connect with him on the most intimate level.

"I'm leaving tomorrow. I didn't want to go without…"

He didn't have to say the rest. She knew what he wanted. What *she* wanted. She could stand here and pretend that it wasn't real or that she didn't want it, but that would be a lie. Tomorrow he would be gone and if she didn't seize this moment she would regret it for the rest of her life.

Could she do that? Risk the damage to her heart?

She pushed the uncertainty away. Her entire adult life she had erred on the side of caution when it came to affairs of the heart… but not tonight.

She didn't wait for him to say anything else or even for him to move. She moved. Reached out to him and took him in her arms.

His mouth came down on hers so quickly she didn't have time to catch her breath. She reached up, let her hands find a home on his broad shoulders.

She didn't need to see his face. She could taste Joe Hennessey...recognized the ridges and contours of his muscular chest and arms. She didn't know how she could have done something as foolish as fall for this man...but she had. There was no changing that fact. The best she could hope for was to salvage some part of her heart after he'd gone.

His fingers moved over her, making her sizzle beneath the silky fabric. Wherever his palms brushed her skin heat seared through her. She couldn't get enough of his touch, couldn't stop touching him. Even the thought of taking her lips from his made her experience something like panic.

No matter what the future held for either of them, they could have this night.

His hands slid down her back, molded to her bottom. She gasped, the sound captured by his lips. He urged her hips against his and she cried out. Ached with such longing that she wasn't sure she could bear it.

Joe held her tightly against him, shook with the incredible sensations washing over him.

He shouldn't have come to her like this. He'd known better. For the past forty-eight hours he'd told himself over and over that she'd done the right thing walking away. It was the best move for all concerned.

But he couldn't leave without kissing her one last time. He'd thought of nothing else every minute he hadn't been attempting to talk himself out of this very moment.

He'd thought about that one kiss they had shared. Of the way her body had reacted to his all those months ago when he'd come to her rescue.

He needed to feel her in his arms. He'd walked away the last time without looking back because she had belonged to another man. That had been a mistake. He should have fought for her. They'd had a connection. He'd felt it. So had she, he'd bet his life on it. But he'd walked away and tried to put her out of his mind.

Impossible.

Spending the past three weeks with her had only convinced him further that they had something special. All they had to do was explore it…let it happen naturally.

He had to make her see that.

She trembled when he reached for the hem of her gown and tugged it up and off. God, he wanted to see her body, to learn every hollow and curve. But the light would ruin everything. He needed her to know who was making love to her tonight. He couldn't let Maddox's face interfere. He crouched down long enough to drag her panties down her legs. The subtle rose scent of her freshly bathed skin took his breath.

As he stood her fingers shook when she struggled to release the buttons of his shirt. He helped, tugging the shirttails out of his trousers and meeting her at the middle button. The sound of her breath rushing in and out of her lungs made him feel giddy.

Together they worked his trousers down to his ankles, then stumbled back onto the bed with the efforts of removing his shoes and kicking free of the trousers.

He peeled off his boxers then lay on the bed next to her. He didn't want to rush this. As badly as he wanted to push between her thighs and enter her right now, he needed to make this night special. Take things slow, draw out the pleasure. Like it was their last night on earth.

He slid his fingers over her breasts, pleasured her nipples, relishing her responsive sounds. Unable to resist, he bent down and sucked one hardened peak. She arched off the mattress, cried out his name. He smiled and gave the other nipple the same treatment just to hear her call out his name again. He loved hearing her voice…so soft and sexy.

He kissed his way down her rib cage, tracing each ridge, laving her soft skin with his tongue. He paid special attention to her belly button. Sweat formed on his body with the effort of restraint. He was so hard it hurt to breathe, but he couldn't stop touching her this way, with his hands, his mouth.

He touched the dewy curls between her legs, teased the channel there and she abruptly stiffened. His body shook at the sounds as she moaned with an unexpected release.

When her body had relaxed he immediately went to work building that tension once more. He nuzzled her breasts, nipped her lips, all the while sliding one finger in and out of her. Her heated flesh pulsed around him, squeezed rhythmically. Soon, very soon he needed to be inside her.

Elizabeth couldn't catch her breath. She needed to touch him all over…needed to have him take her completely. She couldn't bear anymore of this exquisite torture. She couldn't think…couldn't breathe.

She encircled his wrist, held his skilled hand still before he brought her to climax yet again. "No more," she pleaded.

He kissed her lips, groaned as she trailed her fingers over his hardened length. She shuddered with delight at the feel of him. So smooth and yet so firm, like rock gilded with pure silk.

Her breath left her all over again as he moved into position over her. She opened her legs, welcomed his weight. His sex nudged hers and she bit down hard on her lower lip to prevent a cry of desperation.

He thrust into her in one forceful motion. For several seconds she couldn't move or speak. He filled her so completely. The urge to arch her hips was very nearly overwhelming but somehow she couldn't move. She could only lay very, very still and savor the wondrous awareness of being physically joined with Joe.

Eventually he began to move, slowly at first, then long, pounding strokes. The rush toward climax wouldn't be slowed, hard as she fought it. She could feel him throbbing inside her. His full sex grew harder as his own climax roared toward a peak.

They came together, cried out with the intensity of it.

As they lay there afterward, neither able to speak with their lungs gasping for air, Elizabeth understood that she had just crossed a line of no return.

She had allowed Joe Hennessey inside her. She, a doctor, had participated in unprotected sex. But worst of all she'd freely given over her already damaged heart.

"Elizabeth, I've wanted to make love to you since the first time I saw you," he murmured, his lips close to her temple. "No matter where I was, I couldn't close my eyes without seeing you."

Her chest felt tight. A part of her wanted to confess to the same weakness, but that would be to admit that three months ago she'd already disengaged emotionally from David. What did that make her?

She squeezed her eyes shut and blocked the thoughts. She didn't want to think right now. She just wanted to lay here and feel Joe next to her. She wanted to let her body become permeated with the scent and taste of him.

Just for tonight.

"When this is over," Joe said softly, "I want to see where these feelings take us. I don't want to let you go."

When this mission was over…then there would be another. Clarity slammed into her with crushing intensity. And another mission after that. Each time Joe would be gone for days or weeks. He could be killed in some strange place and she would never even know what really happened.

Just like before.

She had known this would be a mistake. She couldn't let herself believe in—depend on—a man who risked so much. She'd already gotten too close to him. Letting it go this far was crazy.

"I can't do this." She scooted away from him and to the edge of the bed. "You should go."

He sat up next to her. It was all she could do not to run away. But she had let this happen. She had to face the repercussions of her actions.

He exhaled a heavy breath, turned to her and began, "When I get back—"

She jerked up from the bed, fury and hurt twisting inside her. "If you come back." She hurled the words at him through the darkness, imagined his face—his *real* face.

He didn't respond immediately, just sat there making no move to get dressed. She couldn't see him really, just the vague outline but she could feel his frustration.

"I will be back, Elizabeth. I won't leave you the way he did."

A new rush of tears burned in her eyes. "How can you make a promise like that? You have no idea if you'll survive this mission much less the next one!"

"Elizabeth, don't do this." He stood, moved toward her, but she backed away.

She was too vulnerable right now. If he touched her again she might not be able to stick by her guns. She just couldn't do this to herself again. It hurt too much.

"I know you don't want me to go," he whispered, his voice silky and more tempting than anything she'd ever experienced.

Don't listen!

She had to be strong.

"I want you to go," she reiterated. "I'm not going to fall in love with another man who can't live outside the lure of danger. I won't let that happen."

She had to get out of here. Nothing he said would change how she felt. She felt around for her gown, found it and quickly jerked it on. The sooner she put some distance between them the better off she would be.

"Maybe it's not too late for you," he said causing her to hesitate at the door. She would not let herself look back. "But," he went on, "it's way too late for me. It's already happened."

She walked out.

A numbness settled over her.

What was he saying?

She shook off his words.

Nothing he said mattered.

She had to protect herself.

This was the only way.

Joe dragged on his clothes and pushed his feet into his shoes. A rock had settled in his stomach. He needed to convince her that they could do this, but she didn't want to listen right now.

A part of him wanted to track her down and make her see this his way. But that would get him nowhere fast.

Maddox had hurt her. She was only protecting herself.

Joe was the one who'd made a mistake.

He should have realized she needed more time. Especially under the circumstances. For God's sake, she'd scarcely gotten through giving him the face of her old lover and learning of the full extent of her former lover's betrayal. How could he have expected her to fall into his arms and live happily ever after?

Because he was selfish. Desperate to have her as his own. But he'd screwed up. Succeeded in pushing her farther away. Regaining that tender ground might very well be impossible.

He walked out of her room, surveyed the dimly lit hall but she was gone. If he wanted to, he could find her. She wouldn't be far away. Maybe in the kitchen or behind one of the closed doors right here in this hall. But he couldn't do that. He had to respect her needs.

Coming here had been his first mistake tonight. He wasn't about to make another. Oddly he couldn't bring himself to regret making love with her. Mistake or not, he refused to regret it for a single moment.

Not in this lifetime.

He stole out the rear exit of her brownstone and into the concealing darkness of the night.

Right now he didn't have time to work this out. He had an assignment that couldn't wait another day.

But when he got back one way or another he intended to sway her to his way of thinking. Whatever it took, he wouldn't give up.

They belonged together.

All he had to do was survive this mission.

He had as many of the facts as was possible to glean from the sparse details they had uncovered. He had the face Elizabeth had given him—his ticket into Maddox's seedy world of betrayal.

He would get this done. He would return to Elizabeth and then he would make her see that he was right.

Maybe she didn't feel as strongly about their relationship as he did, though he suspected she did. But that didn't change a damned thing as far as he was concerned.

He was definitely in love with her.

Chapter Eleven

Elizabeth stared at the tousled sheets on her bed. She'd done it again. Made a huge error in judgment.

She hadn't been able to sleep in here last night. Not with the smell of their lovemaking having permeated every square inch of the room. Even now she could smell the lingering scent of Joe. If she closed her eyes she could recall vividly the way he'd touched her in the dark.

And now he was gone.

She steeled herself against the fear and worry. This was exactly why she hadn't wanted to fall for a man like him again.

Who was she kidding? She'd fallen for him before she'd even known her relationship with David was over. She'd lied to herself, pretended she hadn't felt the things she felt for Joe. Denial was a perfectly human reaction to anything confusing or fearful. Just because she was a trained physician didn't make her any less human.

Or any smarter, it seemed.

Elizabeth quickly dressed, choosing her most comfortable slacks and a pale blue blouse. She needed all the comfort she could get today, including a light hand with makeup. Not that she wore that much anyway, but she just didn't feel up to the extra effort today.

As she exited her bedroom, she refused to think of Joe and the idea that he'd likely begun efforts to infiltrate the enemy. If she did she would only start to worry about where he was and what was happening to him.

Today was the pivotal test of all her work. His face, his mannerisms and speech. All of it would be scrutinized by the group of assassins he needed to fool.

God, what if these evil people had already heard somehow that David was dead?

She couldn't go there…just couldn't do it.

Work. She needed work to occupy her mind.

When she reached the door she remembered her blazer and she hurried back to her room to grab one.

Again the tangled mass of linens tugged at her senses. She got out of there, took the stairs two at a time.

Determined to put last night completely behind her, she opened her front door and stepped out into the day.

The sun gleamed down, warming her face, giving her hope that this day might turn out all right after all.

A new beginning. Another opportunity to do something good and right. Maybe she would never be as smart as she should be in her personal life, but her career could be enough. It had been for a long time now. Why change a game plan that appeared to work?

"Are you ready, Dr. Cameron?"

Elizabeth smiled at Agent Dawson. Nice, safe, quiet Dawson. Like Dr. Newman. The kind of man she should be seeking, but somehow never gravitated toward.

"Yes, I am, Agent Dawson." And it was true. She was ready to move on. And she could as long as she didn't stop long enough to think.

"There's been a change in plans this morning," he commented as they moved toward the vehicles parked at the curb. "I'll need to drive you to the clinic this morning if you don't have any objections."

She shrugged. "No problem." It wasn't like she had plans to go anywhere during the course of the day. If she had lunch she usually ate in her office. Most likely she'd spend what time she had available between patients going over files and finishing up reports.

That was the least glamorous part of her job—paperwork. Not the insurance forms or billing statements prepared by the clinic's accounting staff, but the detailed reports on patient history and recommended procedures as well as results of those performed and updates on follow-up consultations. Lots and lots of reports and analyses.

Elizabeth frowned as she glanced out the car window. Was there some reason he hadn't shared with her that dictated the necessity of an alternate route? This wasn't the way she usually drove to work.

"Agent Dawson." She leaned forward to get a better look at him if he glanced her way in the rearview mirror. "Is there some reason we're going this way rather than my usual route?"

"I can't answer that, ma'am. I have my orders."

Elizabeth leaned back in her seat, but she didn't relax. She had known Agent Craig Dawson for more than a year. Something about his voice didn't mesh with the man she knew. This was wrong somehow.

"Agent Dawson," she ventured hesitantly, "is something wrong?"

He glanced in the rearview mirror for the briefest moment and their eyes met. In that instant she saw his fear, recognized the depth of it.

"I'm sorry, Dr. Cameron," he said, his tone hollow, listless. "They have my family…they're going to kill them if I don't do what they tell me. Please believe I didn't have any choice."

Terror tugged at Elizabeth's sternum. *They.* He had to mean the people who worked with David…the ones to whom he'd sold out his fellow agents.

Her heart bolted into panic mode.

Was he taking her to them?

Or did he plan to kill her himself…in order to save his family?

She moistened her lips and marshaled her courage. "What're you supposed to do, Agent Dawson?"

His uneasy gaze flicked to the rearview mirror once more. "I have to deliver you to the location they specified. That's all." He looked away. "God, I don't want to do this."

"We should call Agent Stark." She rammed her hand into her purse, fished for her cell phone. Her heart pounded so hard she could scarcely think. "He'll know what to do."

Where was her phone? She turned her purse upside down and emptied the contents. She always put it back in her purse before going to bed after allowing it to charge for a couple of hours.

"We can't do that, ma'am."

The full ramifications of the situation struck her. He'd taken her cell phone. His family was being held hostage.

Agent Dawson was no longer her advocate.

"Stop the car, Agent Dawson." Her order sounded dull and carried little force, but she had to try.

His defeated gaze met hers in the rearview mirror once more. "I'm afraid I can't do that, Dr. Cameron."

Panic knotted in her stomach, tightened around her throat. She steeled herself against it, mentally scrambled to consider the situation rationally.

Her movements slow, mechanical, she picked up her belongings one item at a time and dropped them back into her purse. The lip balm she always carried. Hairbrush. Keys. Her attention shifted back to the keys. They could be useful. She tucked the keys into the pocket of her blazer.

She glanced up to make sure Agent Dawson wasn't watching her, then sifted through the rest. Ink pen. Another possible weapon. She slid it into her pocket as well. With nothing else useful, she scooped up the rest and spilled it into her bag.

Okay. She took a deep breath. Get a clean grip on calm and keep it. No matter what happened she needed to keep her senses about her.

She was a doctor. She'd been trained to maintain her composure during life-and-death situations. This was basically the same thing.

Only it was her life on the line.

Searching for a serene memory to assist her efforts she latched on to the sensations from last night. Smells, tastes, sounds of pleasure.

She clung to the recollection of how Joe's skin had felt beneath her palm. The weight of his muscular body atop hers. She trembled as the moments played in her mind. Their bodies connected in the most intimate manner.

But most of all she held on to the last words he'd said to her…he loved her. He hadn't needed to utter those exact words, the message had been clear.

Whether she lived through this day or not, she could hold that knowledge close to her heart. She wished she had told him how she felt. Even if it was a mistake, he'd deserved to know. How was it that fear for one's life suddenly made so many things crystal clear?

She did have deep feelings for Joe. If she were totally honest with herself she would have to say that she loved him. She would also have to admit that it was, without question, a huge mistake. But, under the circumstances, that point seemed moot altogether.

Elizabeth turned her attention back to the passing landscape. She needed to pay attention to their destination. That ability was another thing that no doubt spelled doom for her. Didn't they always blindfold hostages in the movies so they wouldn't know where they were taken? Further proof that the outcome for her would not include a dashing hero and a last-minute escape. She would know too many details to risk her survival.

All the more reason to be prepared.

Another thought occurred to her then. "Agent Dawson." Her voice sounded stark in the car after the long minutes of silence. When his gaze collided with hers in the mirror she went on, "How can you be sure they won't harm your family anyway?"

He didn't answer, except the look in his eyes gave her his answer. He couldn't be sure, but he had to try. His work had brought danger to his family. He had to take whatever risks necessary in an attempt to keep them safe. He wasn't a field operative. He was reacting the only way he knew how.

Elizabeth didn't readily recognize the neighborhood. It wasn't the sort of area anyone would willingly frequent. Dilapidated houses and crumbling apartment buildings. Trash lay scattered in parking lots and along the broken sidewalks. Junked cars as well as newer models, some considerably more expensive than the houses they fronted, lined the street. At this hour of the morning no one appeared to be stirring about. But she didn't have to see any of the residents to guess at the community profile. Poverty-stricken. Desperate.

Every city had its forgotten corners. Areas where the government failed to do enough. Where people survived on instinct and sheer determination.

No one here would care what happened down the street or on the next block. Survival depended upon looking the other way and keeping your mouth shut.

Elizabeth had never known this sort of hopelessness. No one should. She hoped this sad part of life wouldn't be the last thing she ever saw.

The car stopped and Elizabeth jerked to attention. Her gaze immediately roved the three-story building that sat on a corner lot. The windows were boarded up and the roof looked to be missing most of its shingles.

Dawson got out of the car and walked around to her side. He opened the car door and waited for her to get out. Vaguely she wondered what he would do if she refused. Would he shoot her? She didn't think so.

The energy would be wasted. She had no choice any more than he did. Making matters more difficult would serve no purpose. Agent Dawson wasn't her enemy. It was the people inside this ramshackle building who represented the true threat.

She got out of the car and he took her by the arm. She didn't resist, didn't see the point.

He led her to the front entrance and ushered her inside where the condition of the structure was no better than the outside had been.

Though it was daylight outside, the interior was barely lit and only by virtue of the sunlight slipping between the boards on the windows. She wondered if there was any electricity supplying power to the building. Not likely.

Up two flights of stairs and at the end of the hall Dawson hesitated. Elizabeth met his gaze, saw the regret and pain churning there.

"I'm sorry, Dr. Cameron."

The door behind him swung open and a man carrying a large, ugly gun stepped into the hall. He quickly patted down Agent Dawson and removed the weapon he carried in his shoulder holster. Then he did the same to Elizabeth. He ignored the keys and pen.

"This way," he growled.

Dawson held on tightly to her elbow as they moved into the room the man had indicated. She wished she had told Dawson that she knew he was sorry and that she understood, but there hadn't been time.

"Well, well."

Elizabeth's attention darted in the direction of the female voice. Blond hair cut in a short, spiky style, analyzing gray eyes. She looked tough dressed in her skintight jeans and T-shirt. Her arms were muscular as if she worked out with weights. She wore a shoulder holster which held a handgun while she carried a larger, rifle type weapon similar to that of her comrade.

"I finally get to meet sweet Elizabeth," the woman said hatefully.

Elizabeth felt her muscles stiffen. This was *the* woman. She didn't have to be told. The woman referred to her in a way that David had regularly, sweet Elizabeth.

Unflinching, she lifted her chin and stared at the other woman who seemed to tower over her. "Who are you?"

The witch with the guns laughed, boldly, harshly. "I think you know who I am."

Elizabeth ignored Dawson's fingers squeezing her elbow. His concern for her was needless. She doubted either one of them would make it out of here alive.

"You must be the woman David left every time he came home to me," Elizabeth said succinctly. The transformation on the other woman's face let her know her words had prompted the desired result.

Looking ready to kill, the woman strode up to Elizabeth and shoved the barrel of the rifle she carried into Elizabeth's chest. "You think you know something about me, Miss Goody Two-Shoes?"

Elizabeth held her ground despite the terror sending tremor after tremor through her. "I know David never once mentioned you."

The woman's face contorted with anger. Elizabeth braced herself for the fallout. To her surprise the woman's attention shifted to Dawson.

"Get his wife on the line," she said to her accomplice.

Dawson tensed. "I did everything you asked. You said you'd let them go."

"That's right," Elizabeth interjected, her heart aching for the poor man, "you got what you wanted. Let Agent Dawson and his family go."

Dawson looked at her then, his expression trapped somewhere between thankful that his family appeared to be safe for the moment—since he would soon hear his wife's voice—and downtrodden because of what he'd done to Elizabeth.

The woman said nothing to Elizabeth but tossed a cell phone to Dawson.

"Hello?"

The look of relief on his face told Elizabeth that his wife was on the other end of the line.

"You're all right?" he verified. Horror abruptly claimed his expression. "No!" He stared at the woman who'd given him the phone, then at the phone. "What've you done?"

The oxygen evacuated Elizabeth's lungs and the room suddenly tilted. Had they…? Oh, God.

"Don't worry, Mr. CIA Agent," the woman taunted with a wave of her gun, "you're going to join them…right now."

The horrible woman fired two shots. Dawson jerked with the impact, staggered back then collapsed on his side into a twisted heap on the dusty wood floor. The color of blood spread rapidly in a wide circle on his shirtfront.

Elizabeth dropped onto her knees next to him. She rolled him onto his back and assessed the situation.

Before she could attempt to stop the bleeding, the man with the gun hauled her to her feet.

"He'll die!" Elizabeth screamed at him as if he were deaf or stupid.

"That's the point," he said in that low guttural growl of his.

Elizabeth felt the hysteria clawing at the back of her throat. She felt cold and numb. The urge to scream squirmed in her chest.

She thought of the keys in her pocket and how she might be able to use them. But it was no use. She recognized from the location of the wound that nothing she could do in this setting would benefit Agent Dawson.

His family was dead. Maybe he was better off that way, too. He would never have forgiven himself if he'd lived.

Elizabeth swiveled toward the woman standing only a few feet away. "What do you want?" Her voice carried its own kind of malicious intent.

For the first time in her life Elizabeth understood completely how it felt to want to kill someone. If she possessed a weapon she would not hesitate to murder one or both of those holding her hostage.

The woman grinned, an expression straight from hell. "Everything," she said with sinister glee.

The man grabbed Elizabeth's arm again and pushed her toward a door on the other side of the room. "Where are we going?" she demanded, a new kind of fear rushing through her veins.

He cut her a look but said nothing.

The smaller room he shoved her into was empty and just as unkempt as the other one. Before she could turn around he slammed the door shut. She rushed to it, knowing before she twisted the knob that it would be locked.

A surge of relief made her knees weak. At least he hadn't followed her in here.

She moved back from the door, took a moment to gather her wits. Okay, she had to think.

The events of the past few minutes reeled through her mind like a horror flick. She closed her eyes and banished the images. She didn't want to see Dawson's face when he'd heard whatever they did to his wife on the other end of that phone call. She didn't want to see him fall into a dying heap on the floor over and over.

Things like this didn't happen in her life. She was just a doctor. One who worked at a quiet, upscale clinic. She'd never had to deal with the hysteria and insanity of E.R. work. She'd never been exposed to this sort of horror outside a movie theatre.

Several more deep breaths were required before she could stop her body from quaking so violently.

She reached into her pocket. Keys, ink pen. Not much that would help her in this situation.

Okay…think. First she needed to take stock of her situation. She moved to the boarded-up window on the other side of the room. Peered through the cracks between the boards. Nothing. Not a single pedestrian to call to for help, not that she was sure anyone in this neighborhood would be willing to get involved. But maybe someone would call the police if they heard screaming. She glanced toward the door. Of course if she screamed her captors would come running.

She tugged at one of the boards. The wood creaked and shifted but not enough for her to work it loose.

"Damn."

She walked around the room. Surveyed the floor. Looked inside the one other door that opened up to a tiny closet. This room had probably been a bedroom at one time. She looked up at the ceiling. No removable ceiling tiles or attic access doors. Just stained, cracked drywall.

There was no way out of here. She had to face that fact.

She propped against the wall near the window. She couldn't get out the window, but it made her feel better to be near it all the same.

Why hadn't they killed her? There had to be a reason she was still breathing.

The woman with the guns had said she wanted *everything*. What did that mean?

Had David failed to follow through with all the names of the agents she'd given new faces? That was the only marketable asset Elizabeth possessed in this lethal scenario. But why would David betray his country—and her—and then fall down on the job?

Maybe he'd been killed before he could provide the full list. Why then had it taken these goons three months to come looking for the rest?

It didn't make sense.

Did criminal activities ever make sense?

She scrubbed her hands over her face and exhaled loudly. Would Dr. Newman miss her this morning and call her house to see where she was? When he didn't get her would he contact the police?

She didn't think so. He could well assume that she'd had a personal emergency come up. She was an adult after all, one who had recently rebuffed his advances at that. He might not care to pursue the question of where she was this morning.

So what did she do?

Could she just stand here waiting for one of her captors to decide it was time to kill her? Did she dare assume that she was some sort of bargaining chip who would be kept alive for trading purposes?

She just didn't have any experience in this sort of situation. But the one thing she did know was that being a victim, to some extent, was a choice. She could stand here feeling helpless until they came for her or she could devise a way to fight back.

She'd always struggled to reach her goals, never once giving up. She had to do that now, had to find a way to help herself. She might not escape, but she would die trying.

She had nothing to lose by tackling the boards over the window again. That appeared to be her only viable means of possible escape.

After swiping her damp palms against her pants she grabbed hold of a board and pulled with all her might. It didn't budge much, but it did give a little.

Even that little bit gave her hope.

She worked harder, struggled with all her might.

The first board came loose, sending her staggering backward. She barely managed to stay on her feet.

Her heart pounding with anticipation, she laid the board aside and reached for the next one.

She could do this.

She *had* to do this.

Her life depended upon it.

The door suddenly flew open and Elizabeth pivoted to face what would no doubt be one of her captors.

Her heart surged into her throat.

Joe.

She rushed across the room and into his arms. Tears streamed down her cheeks but she didn't care. She was just so damned glad to see him. How had he found her?

She hadn't heard a scuffle. Had he killed those two awful people holding her here?

"Thank God you found me," she murmured against the welcoming feel of his wide shoulders. "I'm so sorry I made you leave last night. We should have made love again."

Last night felt like a lifetime ago now, but she had to tell him the truth now, right this second. She wouldn't leave him hanging another moment.

"You were right, Joe, it's too late for me, too. I love you." She drew back and looked into his eyes. "I should have—"

Her stomach bottomed out and every ounce of relief she'd felt drained away as surely as Agent Dawson's blood had.

She knew those eyes…not contacts…recognized those lips… This wasn't Hennessey…this was…

"David." But he was dead…wasn't he?

Chapter Twelve

Joe's flight landed in Newark, New Jersey, twenty minutes earlier than scheduled. He grabbed his carry-on bag, the only one he'd brought with him and waited for an opportunity to merge into the line of passengers heading for the exit at the front of the plane.

After disembarking he made his way to the terminal exits and hailed a cab. He gave the warehouse address and relaxed into the seat. It was five twenty-two. Thirty minutes from now he would arrive at his rendezvous point and the game would begin.

One call to the man on the ground here in Jersey and his contact had agreed to meet with him at six o'clock.

Ginger was her name.

She'd been expecting to hear from him weeks ago. Lowering his voice and summoning that gravelly tone Maddox used, Joe had explained that his assignment had kept him under deep cover far longer than he'd anticipated, but he was back now. He needed to touch base and get a status on how the operation was proceeding. He'd considered demanding to know why only three agents had been taken out so far but since he didn't know the ultimate reasoning behind that move, he didn't risk it. For all he knew Maddox could have dictated the dates each hit would go down.

As the scenery zoomed past his window Joe's thoughts found their way back to last night. To the way touching her had shaken his entire world. He'd known it would be that way. From the first time he'd seen her, watched her walk across the parking lot at her clinic, he'd sensed she was special. Maybe too special for him. He wasn't at all sure a guy like him deserved a woman like that.

Making love to her last night had fulfilled every fantasy he'd enjoyed since that night months ago, when he'd first held her in his arms to keep her from walking into a trap at her clinic.

Her body had responded to his as if they'd been made for each other. Every touch had ripped away yet another layer of his defenses. He'd spent his entire adult life avoiding commitment on an emotional level. His work made him unreliable in that department. He understood that. Knew with complete certainty that a permanent relationship would be unfair on far too many levels for any woman to tolerate.

But he just hadn't been able to help himself where Elizabeth was concerned. He'd wanted her more than he'd ever wanted any woman. He couldn't recall once ever being this vulnerable to need.

Elizabeth comprehended the difficulty becoming involved with a man like him entailed. She'd clearly made a promise to herself not to risk her heart to any more men like David Maddox. And as much as Joe wanted to argue that he wasn't anything at all like Maddox, he recognized the career-related similarities. Still he wanted nothing more than to convince her to let this thing between them develop naturally. He wanted to make promises. Promises he might not be able to keep.

It was too much to ask. He would be the first to admit to that glaring fact. How could he ask her to give that much?

He couldn't.

She had been right to ask him to leave.

He should never have gone to her like that. She'd already been hurt by one man like him. She deserved the chance to find someone more reliable, more available with whom to share her life.

She deserved that and more. And Calder had to find a way to protect her better. He couldn't let anyone like Maddox near her again.

She'd paid far too much for that mistake.

The taste of her lips abruptly filled Joe and it took every ounce of strength he possessed to push the tender memories away.

He had to focus now.

Staying alive had to be top priority.

Maybe he and Elizabeth didn't have a future together but that didn't mean he couldn't hope.

"Stop here," he told the driver.

The cabbie pulled the taxi over to the curb four blocks from Joe's ultimate destination. He paid the fare and got out. The air he sucked into his lungs felt thick with humidity and the smell of diesel fuel from the huge trucks and trailers still rumbling in the distance down Avenue A. At almost six o'clock things were winding down along this particular warehouse-lined street of Newark's Ironbound community. A few trailers were still being loaded. The sounds of rush-hours traffic from the surrounding streets and avenues mixed with the heavier grumbling of the trucks.

He surveyed the deserted warehouses at the far end of the street where encroaching residential developments made the old standing structures ripe for condo-izing. Not exactly a picturesque view for perspective owners.

Dressed in jeans and boots and a T-shirt beneath an open button-down chambray shirt Joe blended well with the warehouse crews headed home for the night. He used that to his benefit and moved easily toward the rendezvous point.

He fell into "Maddox" stride without thought. Focused his energy on giving off a confident vibe. This meeting was his and Ginger's and anyone else planning to be there needed to know that. Maddox never let another human being intimidate him. From watching the videos of a number of his interrogations he liked belittling his assets. Though all agents took that approach to some degree Maddox went further than most. He appeared to get off on degrading those he considered lesser forms of life, which appeared to be most other humans.

The abandoned warehouse where Ginger waited looked in less than habitable condition. He took a final moment to get into character then went inside. He carried the 9 mm Beretta in his waistband at the small of his back and a backup piece in an ankle holster. His preferred weapon of choice was a Glock but for this mission he needed to carry what Maddox would.

"It's about time."

Joe settled his gaze on the woman with blond spiky hair and immediately recognized her as Ginger from the surveillance photos on file at the Agency.

"Patience has never been one of your strong suits." He kept his gaze fastened on hers. No averting his eyes, no letting her read anything that Maddox wouldn't display in this situation.

Ginger sashayed over to him, a high-powered rifle hanging down her back from a shoulder strap. "Did you miss me?" she asked as she slid her arms up and around his neck.

He gifted her with a Maddox smile. "Occasionally."

She kissed him and he kissed her back, using all the insights that Elizabeth had shared with him. Aggressive, invasive. Ginger appeared to like it. Maybe too much.

He set her away. "We have business to attend to," he said in an icy growl that made her eyes widen in surprise. He didn't analyze her reaction in an attempt to prevent any outward response himself.

She inclined her head and studied him. "You're right. We've kept him waiting too long already."

With that ominous announcement she pivoted on her heel, the weapon on her shoulder banging against her hip, and strode toward the freight elevator.

Joe followed. From the intelligence the Agency had gathered there was at least one more scumbag working with this woman. Her known accomplice was male, twenty-seven or -eight, and seriously scruffy-looking. But then, he watched the woman pull down the overhead gate that served as a door and set the lift into motion, that didn't surprise him after meeting the enigmatic Ginger in person. She looked about as unsavory as they came. The third man was the unknown factor, but Joe imagined that he would be every bit as sleazy.

Maddox's taste had definitely altered. Of course a field operative couldn't always be selective when working undercover. However, Maddox had, so far as they had determined, continued his alliance with these three well after the mission ended. If Joe's conclusions were correct, Maddox had used at least two of this group to orchestrate the hits on his fellow agents. The question was, for whom? The why was about money. It didn't take a rocket scientist to figure out that part.

Too bad for Maddox. A guy couldn't take his hefty bank account to hell with him.

The upward crawl came to an abrupt, jarring halt on the third floor and his guide shoved the door up and out of the way. The third level appeared to be nothing but a wide-open vacant space. What could be an additional storage room or office stood at the far end and was separated from the larger space by a single door.

She glanced over her shoulder. "Stay here."

Joe snagged her by the elbow and wheeled her around to face him. "This sounds a lot like insubordination, *baby,*" he offered, his tone at once sensual and accusing.

Again her eyes widened in something like surprise, kindling his instincts once more and sending him to a higher state of alert.

"Just following orders," she said with a shrug before pulling free of his hold and heading toward the door on the other side of the space.

Joe's instincts were humming. Something was off here. A glitch he couldn't quite name. But he understood that the undercurrents he felt were tension filled. The surprise he'd seen in Ginger's eyes. Had she recognized something a little off with her former lover?

There was always the possibility that she and her accomplice had heard that Maddox was dead but Joe doubted that. The info had been kept within Director Calder's realm alone.

Intelligence indicated that the group had been putting out feelers as to Maddox's location.

There was every reason to believe that the two leaders of this little group, Ginger and her male counterpart, Fahey, had orchestrated the three assassinations thus far. Whatever their motivation, the two wanted to hook up with their source, David Maddox, once more. There was nothing on the third party.

Maybe it was the physical relationship between Ginger and Maddox or maybe it was simply a matter of needing the rest of the names.

Joe would be the first one to admit that he'd been surprised by Maddox's duplicity. It wasn't that he hadn't suspected the guy was fully capable of that kind of betrayal. He'd simply believed him to be devoted to his work and his country, if not the people in his personal life, specifically Elizabeth Cameron.

Maybe that sticking point had been the catalyst for Joe's determination to prove that Maddox had betrayed not only Elizabeth but his country.

Almost immediately after he'd started his own investigation, one week after the first assassination, intelligence had started to pick up on activity from this group. Joe had known what that indicated.

That's when Joe had gone to Calder with his suspicions. He'd bypassed his immediate supervisor, Director Allen, and laid all his suspicions on the table for the big dog.

Allen wasn't too damned happy about it. But it had gotten things rolling. Once Calder was hooked, Allen had jumped in with both feet.

Joe hadn't really cared whether Allen got on board or not. All he'd needed was Calder's blessing.

He'd gotten that.

He moved to attention when the door opened and Ginger sauntered back into the main room where he waited.

A figure appeared in the doorway behind her and it took a full five seconds for Joe's brain to assimilate what his eyes saw.

Maddox.

He should have known, Joe thought grimly.

Faking his own death would be the perfect way to get off the hook when he had what he needed.

"It's like looking in a mirror," Maddox said as he came closer.

"Yeah," Ginger agreed.

Fury whipped though Joe. "You betrayed your own people, Maddox."

Maddox shrugged. "Everybody has to retire sometime. I always believed in cashing out when stocks are the highest."

Joe shook his head. "I hate to offer a cliché, Maddox, but the truth is you're not going to get away with it."

The sick smile that Maddox was known for slid across his face. "I already have, Hennessey, or hadn't you noticed?"

Maddox inclined his head and Ginger took a bead on Joe, dead center of his chest.

"You can't do that here!"

Joe's gaze moved beyond Maddox.

Now the puzzle was complete.

Director Kurt Allen.

What do ya know? The third party was an inside man.

He'd known Allen was a bastard but he'd thought that was just his personality.

"We have to stick with the plan," Allen snapped. "No mistakes, Maddox." Allen glanced at Joe but quickly averted his gaze.

Maddox didn't like being chastised in front of a former colleague. "This is my op," he snarled. "These are my people. They follow my commands."

"A whole army of one, huh, Maddox?" Joe couldn't resist the dig. The only player on Maddox's team he'd seen so far was the woman. Allen didn't count as a soldier. Joe hoped the dig would get him what he needed to know where the others were and what they were up to, but asking wouldn't likely work out. He'd have to goad it out of the two traitors.

Maddox's furious gaze landed on Joe. "You don't have any idea who I've got working for me, Hennessey, so don't even try."

"Where's your boy Fahey?"

"He's babysitting your sweetie pie," Ginger sneered.

A rush of fear shook Joe but the rage that followed hot on its heels obliterated any hint of the more vulnerable emotion. He fixed his gaze on Maddox. "If anything happens to her you're going to be in need of a second resurrection."

Allen scoffed. "Why would we let anything happen to her? She's what all of this has been about."

Confusion momentarily gained a little ground over his fury. "What the hell are you talking about? This bastard—" he indicated Maddox "—has been killing off our people."

It was Maddox's turn to laugh now, sending Joe's rage right back to the boiling point. That scumbag was a dead man.

"We have no interest," Allen explained with enormous ego, "in killing off recycled agents. What we want is Dr. Cameron."

"We already have a number of excellent surgeons," Maddox added, "but not one of her caliber. Our wealthier clients deserve only the best. She is the best."

In his line of work Joe had come across the slave trade in most every imaginable walk of life, but this was definitely a first.

"You intend to make her work for you," he restated. "Giving rich criminals new faces."

"And fingerprints," Allen said smugly. "We're even perfecting a way to corrupt DNA, make it unreliable. Amazing, isn't it?"

Joe had heard reports on start-up activities like this. Clinics in obscure places attempting to create the ultimate in escapism. New faces, new finger-prints, even new DNA.

It was a damned shame the Agency's own people were working against them.

"It's amazing all right," Joe allowed. "Too bad neither of you lowlifes is going to see it become a reality."

Ginger took aim once more. "Do you want me to get this over with now?"

Joe's fingers itched to go for his own weapon but that would only get him killed. He needed a distraction.

"You know she'll refuse," Joe tossed out there just to buy some time. But he was right. No way would Elizabeth willingly do this.

Maddox shrugged. "She'll come around, Hennessey. You know the techniques."

The thought of Elizabeth being tortured physically or mentally ripped him apart inside.

"She really thought you loved her," he said to Maddox in hopes of stirring some sentimental feelings.

Ginger laughed. "He doesn't love anybody."

Maddox turned his face toward her, smiled approvingly.

"Then I guess it won't matter to either of you that she's carrying your child."

The lie did the trick.

Ginger's fire-ready stance wavered for a fraction of a second.

Just long enough for Joe to react.

He whipped out his 9 mm and fired twice. Ginger dropped. Maddox and Allen dove for the floor.

Maddox was the first to return fire.

Joe rolled to the left. Pulled off another round, capped Allen in the forehead before he'd gotten a grip on his own weapon.

Maddox started firing. Didn't let up.

Joe rolled, curled and twisted to avoid being hit. With no cover it was the only choice he had.

Maddox disappeared through the door on the far end of the room.

Joe scrambled to his feet and lunged in that direction.

He burst through the door just in time to see Maddox going out the window.

Fire escape.

Damn.

At the window a spray of bullets kept Joe from following the route Maddox had taken.

With the last shot still echoing in the air he risked a look out the window. Maddox was halfway down.

Joe muttered a curse and propelled himself out onto the uppermost landing.

He ducked three shots.

That made sixteen.

In the few seconds it would take Maddox to replace his clip, Joe rushed downward. One flight of rusty metal steps, then another.

Bullets pinged against metal, forcing Joe to zig-zag as he plunged down the next flight. He got off two rounds, gaining himself a few seconds' reprieve.

Maddox hit the pavement in the rear alley, landing on his feet and bolting into a dead run.

Joe was three seconds behind him.

His heart pumped madly, sending much needed adrenaline through his veins.

But he had the advantage from this angle.

Problem was if he killed Maddox he might not find Elizabeth until it was too late.

He needed the bastard alive.

Maddox was likely counting on that.

Joe stopped. Spread his legs shoulder width apart and took aim.

The first bullet whizzed right by Maddox's left ear.

The second closer still.

Maddox skidded to a halt. "Okay!" he shouted. "You made your point."

Though he held up both hands in a gesture of surrender, Joe wasn't taking any chances.

"Place your weapon on the ground, Maddox. Now!" Joe eased toward him, keeping a bead on the back of his head.

"All right. All right." He started to lower his

weapon, bending at the knees in order to crouch down close enough to lay the Beretta on the ground.

Ten feet, eight. Sweat beaded on Joe's forehead as he moved closer still.

Just as Maddox's weapon reached shoulder level he dropped and rolled.

Joe almost fired, but hesitated.

That split second of hesitation cost him every speck of leverage he'd gained.

"Looks like we have an impasse," Maddox said from his position on the ground. Though he lay on his back he'd leaned upward from the waist just enough to get a perfect bead on Joe's head.

Joe shrugged nonchalantly. "The way I see it, if we both end up dead, then there won't be any report for me to file."

Maddox grinned. "You always were a cocky SOB. But this time you've met your match."

"I don't think so." Joe's trigger finger tightened. "Now put down your weapon before I have to kill you."

"A good agent never gives up his weapon, Hennessey."

The explosion of the bullet bursting from the chamber was deafening in the long, deserted alley.

The hit dead center.

Chapter Thirteen

Elizabeth crouched in the darkest corner of the room. She squeezed the keys in her hand, letting the bite of metal keep her senses sharp.

David was alive.

The son of a bitch.

Fury boiled up inside her, leaving a bitter burn in her throat.

For weeks after his death she had wished she could have spoken to him one last time before he died. If she'd only had the opportunity to apologize for her impatience and frustration with his work. As dedicated as she had always been to her own work, how could she grow disgruntled about his loyalty to the job? And that was exactly what she'd done. She had used a double standard. It was okay for her to work long hours seven days a week, month in, mouth out, but when he failed to show for weeks on end she'd behaved petulantly.

She'd kidded herself and pretended they were two of a kind and his long absences didn't bother her. But they had. To say otherwise was a lie.

So when she heard about his death she'd tortured herself for endless nights. Thinking of all the things she should have said.

All that energy…all that emotion wasted on a man who wasn't worth the time it took to tell him to get lost.

If only she'd known just what a monster he was she might have killed him herself.

Okay, maybe that was an exaggeration.

But she wanted desperately for him to pay for what he had done. He could rot in prison for the rest of his life and she wasn't sure that would be punishment enough. Yet execution was far too quick and merciful.

Elizabeth closed her eyes and cleared her mind. She couldn't be distracted by her hatred and bitterness toward David. She had to focus. Finding a way to escape the man holding her was the only hope she had of saving Joe.

She knew the meeting location.

All she needed was her freedom.

Her fingers tightened around the keys once more.

If she called him in here by crying out in pain as if she were sick, she could…

Well, she wasn't sure what she would do but she could make it up as she went.

God, she prayed, *please don't let him kill Joe.*

If Joe died…there were so many things she wanted to say to him. Too late…just like before.

Determination roared through her. No. She wouldn't let this happen to her again.

She had to do something.

When David had died there had been nothing she could do. Considering what she knew now she was glad. But this was different. Joe was a good guy and she loved him.

Why was it she couldn't do anything personal right? It always seemed as if she went about her relationships backward or sideways or something.

Deep breath.

She could do this.

Pushing to her feet she gathered her courage and prepared to make her move.

As a doctor she knew his most vulnerable spots. His eyes. The base of the throat. Then, of course, there was always the old reliable scrotum.

Another deep breath.

As she exhaled that lungful of air she cried out at the top of her lungs.

She doubled over, moaned and cried, summoning her most painful memories in an effort to make it sound real.

The door burst inward.

"What the hell is wrong with you?"

Elizabeth wailed again, held her stomach as if the pain were so intense she could do nothing else.

He grabbed her by the arm and tried to pull her up. "I said, what's wrong with you, bitch?"

"God, I don't know." She moaned long and low.

He slung the rifle over his shoulder. "Stand up where I can look at you."

"Ohhhhhh!" With that savage cry she came up with her hand, stabbed the key to her Lexus into his right eye.

He screamed.

His grip on her arm tightened.

She tried to get free.

Couldn't.

His fingers wrenched her arm painfully. The keys flew across the floor.

"Don't move!" He held his left hand over his eye. But he kept her close with the other. "I could kill you!" he snarled like a wounded animal.

Her heart thudded so hard she couldn't draw in a breath. She had to get loose.

Then she remembered her one other weapon.

Her free hand went into her pocket. Her fingers curled around the ink pen.

There was only one way to get away from this man.

She reared her arm back and brought it down hard, shoving the ink pen into the soft tissue at the base of his throat.

He released her. Grabbed at his throat as he frantically gasped for air.

She bolted for the door.

He grabbed her by the waist.

She screamed, tried to twist free.

His weight slammed into her back and they went down together.

She landed in a sprawl on the floor with him atop her.

His fingers curled around her throat. She tried to buck him off. Tried to roll. But he was too heavy. Horrible gasping sounds came from his throat as he struggled to get air past the hole she'd made. Blood soaked into the neck of his T-shirt, dripped down his cheek.

The pressure on her throat cut off her airway. She bucked and gasped. Pulled at his arms. No good.

Blackness swam before her eyes.

Desperate, she clawed at his face. At his injured eye and then at his throat.

He howled and fell off her.

She scrambled away from him. Clambered to her feet and raced toward the door.

She didn't slow or look back until she was out of the small house and on the street.

Hysteria slammed into her full throttle. She stood in the middle of the street and turned all the way around. Where was she?

She'd been blindfolded as she was brought here. The drive had been hours long. She'd dozed off once. She had no idea where she was.

Her gaze landed on a vehicle up the street and she ran in that direction until she could make out the license plate.

New Jersey.

The Garden State.

New Jersey?

The air raging in and out of her lungs, she stood there and tried to think. Avenue A. She'd heard that location mentioned. Warehouse.

A phone. She needed a phone—911. Help. She needed help.

The low drone of an automobile engine sounded behind her. She spun around and her heart leaped. Help!

She ran toward the car. Waved her arms frantically. "Help me! I need the police!"

The car sped forward, hurried past her. The elderly female driver stared wide-eyed at her.

"Help!" Elizabeth cried once more.

It was no use. The woman drove away as fast as she could. Elizabeth looked down at herself then. Blood was smeared on the front of her pale blue blouse. Her hair was likely disheveled. No wonder the woman didn't stop.

Panic slid around her throat like a noose. A crashing sound had her pivoting toward the door of the house she'd escaped.

The sound hadn't come from there.

Thank God.

A phone. She pushed the hair back from her face. Concentrate, Elizabeth. She needed a phone.

She rushed toward the next house. There wasn't a vehicle in the driveway. Please, please let someone be home.

Balling her bloody fist she banged on the door. "Is anyone home?" She banged harder. "Please, I need to use your phone. It's an emergency. Please."

No one was home. If they were, fear kept them from answering the door.

She rushed back out to the street, looked both ways for a driveway with a car in it.

There had to be someone home, car or no car.

Elizabeth rushed from house to house, pounded on door after door.

Finally a door opened. An elderly man stood on the opposite side of the threshold.

"Can't you read?" he groused.

Elizabeth blinked, uncertain what he meant. She tried to calm her respiration. Tried to make herself think rationally.

"See!" He tapped a sigh hanging next to his door. No solicitation.

"No!" She stepped into the path of the closing door. "I need help. I need the police."

He seemed to really look at her then. Blinked behind the thick lenses of his glasses.

"What happened to you?"

"Please," she pleaded. "I need to call the police."

His gaze narrowed in suspicion and for a moment, she feared he wasn't going to let her inside. Finally he backed up, gestured for her to come in.

He quickly surveyed his porch and yard. "Is somebody after you?"

She shook her head. "No, I don't think so." She looked around the room. "I need to use your phone."

He shuffled toward the kitchen. "It's in here."

Elizabeth rushed past him, almost knocking him over. She didn't take the time to apologize. She had to warn Joe.

Her first instinct was to call 911. But the police might not take her word for what was happening. And she didn't have the exact location. The Agency would surely know Joe's plan for connecting with his contact.

She punched in the number she'd learned by heart long ago. A voice answered on the first ring.

"I need to speak with Director Calder." Elizabeth ID'd herself using the code name and number she'd been given when she first agreed to work with the Agency.

When Director Calder's voice came across the line Elizabeth felt the sting of tears. Thank God.

She explained about David and warned that Joe was walking into a trap somewhere in the vicinity of Avenue A here in New Jersey.

The phone cut out.

"What did you say?" She'd missed whatever Director Calder had said.

He repeated, but again the phone started cutting out and she only got a word here and a word there.

She turned to the owner of the house. "Is there something wrong with your phone?"

In the moments it took him to answer, fear surged into her throat. What if she hadn't completely disabled her captor? What if he was out there attempting to tamper with the phone line? Her heart pounded erratically.

"Damn thing won't hardly hold a charge anymore. Just put her back in the cradle for a minute and she'll be fine."

"Director Calder?" she shouted into the mouthpiece of the receiver but the line was dead.

She depressed the talk button again and again. "You're sure that's all it is?"

The old man nodded. "It's the only one I got.

Being cordless lets me use it all around the house but lately it won't hold a charge for long. I guess I left it out of the cradle too long today."

Elizabeth stuck the phone back into its cradle and took two deep, calming breaths. She'd made the call. Even though she didn't know what Calder had said, he'd gotten all she needed to tell him. He would ensure help got to where Joe was supposed to meet his contact.

"You need to wash up or something?" the old man asked. He looked at her face and then her hands. "Your throat's all red and swollen. You sure you're okay, lady?"

She shuddered and considered all the diseases she could catch with that horrible man's blood all over her.

"I'd like to wash up," she managed to get past the lump in her throat. Her body shook so hard she could barely stay vertical. She recognized the symptoms. The receding adrenaline. She'd have to be careful about shock. She'd been through an ordeal.

"Down the hall." He gestured to the hall at her left.

She nodded. "Thank you."

Her legs as weak as a toddler taking her first steps, she staggered to the bathroom.

"Sweet Lord." Her reflection was not a pretty sight. Her hair was a mess. Her face had a few smears of blood but her blouse was the worst. And her throat was red and swollen. Her bloody blouse was even torn.

She shuddered again, wondered if the man who'd been holding her captive was laying in that other house dying. She should call 911.

Being quick about it, she thoroughly washed her hands and face. She ran her fingers through her hair and sighed. That was the best she could do. Before leaving the bathroom she said one more urgent prayer for God to watch over Joe.

Please let him be safe.

When she returned to the living room the old man was still in the kitchen.

"Thought I'd make you some tea," he said as she joined him there.

"Thank you." She nodded to the phone. "May I try your phone again?"

He shrugged. "Probably won't do you any good but you can try."

She picked up the phone and punched in the three digits. The operator answered and she explained about being held captive and injuring her captor to escape. She verified the address with the old man fretting over the tea cups and then hung up.

The police and paramedics would be here soon.

"Thank you," Elizabeth said as she took the tea he offered. "I'm Elizabeth Cameron." She sipped her tea and sighed. The heat felt good drenching her raw throat.

"Rosco Fedder." He sweetened his tea, stirring it thoughtfully. "Sounds like you had yourself a fright, Missy."

She nodded. "More than you can know." That was certainly the truth. She darn sure couldn't tell him that the CIA was involved. He probably wouldn't believe her anyway.

By the time she'd finished her tea she felt a little less shaky. She couldn't stop worrying whether or not Joe was all right. Maybe she should call Director Calder again. The sound of sirens intruded into her thoughts and drew her to the front door.

"They're here." Her voice came out small and shaky in spite of her much calmer state.

Rosco joined her at the door. "You think that fellow survived?"

Dread welled in her belly. "I don't know." But she wasn't worried about the awful man who'd been holding her hostage. She worried about Joe. Had the CIA been able to get help to him in time?

"I'm going over there," she told Rosco. "Thank you for your help."

"That's what neighbors do, lady," he let her know. "They help one another. Most any of the folks in this neighborhood would've done the same if they'd been home. I'm the token old man 'round here. 'Bout the only one retired."

She managed a smile for her Good Samaritan and walked out to the street. Exhaustion made her feet feel as if they weighed a ton each. But she didn't stop until she'd reached the front walk where three police cruisers and an ambulance were parked.

A sedan pulled over to the curb drawing her attention beyond the fray of uniformed personnel rushing about.

The driver's side door opened and a man emerged.

Terror exploded in her chest.

David.

Elizabeth started to run back toward Mr. Fedder's house. Her heart threatened to burst out of her chest but she didn't slow, just kept running.

"Elizabeth!"

She felt her feet stop beneath her, almost causing her to fall forward.

"Elizabeth! It's me, Joe!"

Her whole body quaking like mad, she slowly turned around in time for him to skid to a stop only a couple of feet away.

"Honey, it's me, Joe."

Hope tugged at her. It was Joe's voice. But the face…

Her gaze settled on his and her heart leaped with joy.

The most beautiful blue eyes stared back at her.

"Joe!" She threw herself against him. His big strong arms closed in around her.

"I told you I'd be back," he murmured close to her ear.

And he hadn't let her down.

She drew back and looked into his eyes again. She wanted to tell him the truth…that she loved him despite her best efforts not to.

But would love ever be enough with a dangerous man like Joe Hennessey?

Chapter Fourteen

Elizabeth slipped on her surgical gown then scrubbed up. As she dried her hands and arms she studied her reflection. Her throat was still bruised but she'd get over it.

Incredibly the man who'd done that damage had survived and the Agency hoped to garner much needed information from him. Elizabeth didn't care how useful he could be to the Agency as long as he spent the rest of his life behind bars...far, far away from her.

She'd been stunned to learn that killing off the agents had been a ploy to lure her into a situation, both as a suspect and as an asset to be protected. David had wanted to steal her away in such a manner that an Agency operative, namely Joe Hennessey, would be blamed for her disappearance and ultimate loss. No one would ever be the wiser that David was alive and he would have Elizabeth to use in his new posh escape clinic. She would have been a prisoner, giving sleazy, however wealthy, criminals new faces in exchange for living another day.

How could she have been so completely fooled by David?

"Dr. Cameron."

Elizabeth hauled her attention back to the here and now, and away from those disturbing thoughts. "Yes."

"The patient refuses to be prepped for anesthesia until after he speaks with you."

Elizabeth sighed. "I'll be right there." She'd been through this routine before.

With the same patient as a matter of fact.

She breezed into the O.R. and strode straight up to the operating table.

"What seems to be the problem, Mr. Hennessey?" She glared down at him, resisting the urge to tap her foot.

He looked around the room at the Agency's specialized team who waited to begin. His gaze lit back on Elizabeth's. "I really need to speak with you alone."

Elizabeth rolled her eyes and huffed her exasperation. "Clear the room please."

When the last of the four had moved into the scrub room, Elizabeth, keeping her hands where they wouldn't get contaminated, glared down at her patient.

"I just wanted you to know that I didn't mean to take advantage of you."

She did not want to talk about that night again. In the past three days they'd scarcely seen each other and when they had he'd wanted to apologize for making love to her. How was that for making a girl feel like she was loved? Not once had he mentioned having treaded into that four-letter territory.

So, of course, neither had she.

It was for the best, she supposed. He would go back to his superspy world and she would return to her work.

No harm. No foul.

They were both alive.

That was the most important thing. Right?

Funny thing was, every time she asked herself that question she got no answer.

"That night—"

She held up a sterile hand. "Stop it, please. I don't ever want to talk about that night again." She hoped she managed to keep the truth out of her eyes but she couldn't be sure. The way he scrutinized her face she doubted she hid much from him.

"I guess I can understand how you feel." He heaved out a big breath.

Elizabeth watched his sculpted chest rise and fall with the action. She wanted to touch him so badly that it literally hurt.

But that would be a mistake.

Whatever crazy connection they had shared during those stressful weeks was best forgotten.

"Just give me back my face, Doc." His gaze connected fully with hers and some unreadable emotion reached out to her, made her ache all the more. "I guess that'll have to be enough."

Elizabeth called in the team and within moments they had lapsed into a synchronized rhythm.

As Joe slipped deep into induced sleep she surveyed the face she'd given him. This was the last time she would see David Maddox's face. And she was glad.

She poised, scalpel in hand, over the patient and took a deep breath. "Let's get this done."

ELIZABETH CLOSED the door of her office and collapsed into her chair. She was completely exhausted. She just couldn't understand what was wrong with her. No one could claim she didn't get enough sleep. She slept like the dead. Eight to ten hours every night! It was incredible.

And food. She ate like a wrestler bulking up to meet his weight requirements.

As she sat there marveling over her strange new zest for sleep and food, realization hit her right between the eyes.

She was late for her period. Only about ten days and

that wasn't completely uncommon. Her cycles never had been reliable. She'd considered birth control pills years ago in order to regulate herself but the risks for a woman her age, though she didn't smoke, were just not worth the bother. Condoms had always worked.

But she and Joe hadn't used a condom.

Mortification dragged at her as if the earth's gravity had suddenly cubed itself.

She was thirty-seven years old. A doctor at that. And she could very well be pregnant by *mistake!*

A kind of giddiness abruptly replaced her mortification.

A baby could be…nice.

Anticipation fizzed inside her. Okay, better than nice. A baby could be amazing!

She had to know.

Elizabeth shot to her feet.

She needed a pregnancy test.

Now.

She rushed out of the clinic without a word to anyone. It was her lunch break anyway. She could do what she wanted. Didn't need anyone's permission.

As she settled behind the wheel of her Lexus she considered the attitude she'd just taken.

Maybe she was changing.

What do you know? She might just like this new feeling of liberation. All work and no play had turned into drudgery.

She drove straight to the nearest pharmacy and bought the test. She couldn't bear to wait until she got back to her office, besides she wanted privacy from her colleagues.

Since she was a doctor the pharmacist gladly allowed her to use the employee restroom in the rear of the store.

Her fingers trembling, Elizabeth opened the box and followed the simple instruction. Then she closed the lid on the toilet and sat down to wait.

Joe popped into her thoughts. If she was pregnant, should she tell him?

She chewed her lip. If she did, he would want to be a part of the child's life. Was that a good thing?

Maybe not.

But how could she not tell him?

Elizabeth groaned. More dilemmas.

Anger lit inside her. As soon as the restoration surgery on his face was complete she'd been ushered away from the borrowed clinic. She hadn't even been allowed to stay to see him through recovery.

Director Calder had refused to give her an update on Joe the two times she'd called.

And in the four weeks that had passed she hadn't heard from him once. Joe, not Calder. He hadn't called, hadn't come by. Nothing.

Obviously when he decided to move on he didn't look back.

It was for the best she knew.

But that didn't make it hurt any less.

She'd shed a few tears, cursing herself every time.

Heck, she'd even forced herself to go on a few dates to try and put him out of her mind entirely. But nothing ever worked.

There was just no denying the truth.

She loved him and her heart would not let her forget.

The minute hand on the wall clock moved to the five. It was time.

Holding her breath she picked up the stick and peered at the results.

Positive.

A thrill went through her.

She was pregnant!

Shoving the box and the telltale test stick into the trash, she struggled for calm. Bubbles of excitement kept bobbing to the surface, making her want to alternately laugh and cry. Don't lose it, she warned. Keep it together. She had patients to see this afternoon. She could completely freak out when she got home tonight.

After washing her hands she made her way back to the front of the drugstore, thanked the pharmacist who studied her suspiciously, then hurried to her car.

She didn't drive straight back to the clinic. She was ravenous. Two drive-thrus later and she had what her heart—stomach actually—desired. Two quarter-pounder cheeseburgers, mega fries and an Asian salad with an extra pack of dressing.

The girls in reception gawked at her as she passed through on the way to her office with her armload of bags. She just smiled and kept going. When she'd gotten into her office and closed the door she dumped her load on her desk and relaxed into her chair. After she ate all this she would surely need a nap. She glanced at her schedule. Not going to happen. Oh well, she'd make up for it tonight.

Still a stickler for neatness, she arranged her lunch on the burger wrapper, with the salad bowl anchoring one corner. The first bite made her groan with pleasure. What was it about being pregnant that made food taste so good?

She would have to get a handle on her diet…just not today.

A tap on her door distracted her from her salad. She frowned. If Dr. Newman asked her to go out with him again she was just going to have to tell him that it would be unethical. Their working relationship prevented her from pursing a personal one with him. That should do the trick without hurting his feelings.

"Yes."

The door opened and the next bite never made it to her mouth.

Joe Hennessey, in all his splendor, from that sexy jawline to that perfect nose, waltzed in.

"They told me that you were having lunch." He glanced at the smorgasbord laid out in front of her. "Looks like there might be enough for me to join you."

Elizabeth snatched up the ever present bottle of water on her desk and washed a wad of fries down.

"What do you want, Hennessey?"

He hadn't contacted her in four weeks. The director of the CIA had refused to give her an update on his condition. How dare he show up here now!

The positive results of the pregnancy test flashed in front of her eyes and another wave of giddiness swept over her. She clamped her mouth shut. Couldn't say a word about that until she knew why he was here. And maybe not even then.

He walked up to her desk but didn't sit down. "I should have called you."

That was a start. "Yes, you should have." She nibbled on a fry. She would die before she'd tell him how lonely she'd been. How badly she'd yearned to have him in her bed.

He bracketed his waist with his hands and took a deep breath. "The truth is I didn't want to see you or even talk to you until I was me again."

Stunned, she dropped the fork back into her salad bowl. "I'm not sure I'm following," she said cautiously but she knew what he meant. He wanted her to see him when they talked...*his* face.

He leaned forward, braced his hands on her desk. She inhaled the clean, slightly citrusy scent that was uniquely Joe Hennessey. Her gaze roved his face. Every detail was just as it was before.

Damn she was good.

Elizabeth blinked. Chastised herself for staring. Since he hadn't answered her question he'd obviously paused to take notice of her staring.

She cleared her throat and squared her shoulders. "You're going to have to explain what you mean, Agent Hennessey."

"Don't play games with me, Elizabeth," he warned, those blue eyes glinting with what some might consider intimidation. But she knew him better now. That was his predatory gleam. And she was his prey...he wanted her.

"Really, Hennessey, you should be more specific."

"I love you, Elizabeth. I can't sleep. I can't eat. I miss you. I need to be with you."

I...I...I, was this all about him? Let him sweat for a bit.

She shrugged indifferently. "I've been sleeping fine." She glanced at the food in front of her. "Eating fine as well."

He straightened, threw up his hands. "What do you want me to do? Beg?"

That could work, she mused wickedly.

"No," she told him to his obvious relief.

He eased one hip onto the edge of her desk and popped a French fry into his mouth. "Then tell me what you want, Elizabeth. I'm desperate here."

His work was her first concern. But she would never ask him to give up his career.

"I don't think we could ever work, Joe," she confessed. She looked directly into those gorgeous blue eyes. "You know the reasons."

He downed a swig of her water and grimaced. "What if I told you I'd gone off field duty?"

She froze, her heart almost stopped stone still. "What did you say?" She prayed she hadn't heard wrong.

"I'm taking a position with a new agency, one that compiles intelligence from all the other agencies and prepares reports for the president. I'd tell you more about it but it's top secret." He grinned. "I'm officially a desk jockey. Is that safe enough for you?"

She shook her head. Afraid to believe. "You can't do that for me. You have to do it for you."

He reached for her hand, engulfed it in his long fingers. "I did it for us, Elizabeth." He peered deeply into her eyes. "And just so you know, even if you kick me out, I'm not going back to field work. I'm done with that. So what's it gonna be?"

Elizabeth jumped to her feet and stretched across her desk to put her arms around his neck. "Yes!" She smiled so wide she was sure it looked more like a goofy grin.

His brows drew together in a frown. "Yes what?"

She knew he was teasing by the sparkle of mischief in his eyes. "Yes, I'll marry you, you big dummy."

A grin widened on his sexy mouth. "Well, now." He reached down and nipped her lips. "I guess that means you're going to make an honest man out of me."

"Actually…"

He kissed her and for a few moments all other thought ceased. There was only the taste and heat of his mouth. God she had missed him. Never wanted to be away from him again.

She drew back just far enough to look into his eyes. "Actually," she reiterated, "I thought I'd make this child I'm carrying legally yours. You okay with that?"

It was Joe's turn to be stunned. "A father? I'm going to be a father?"

Elizabeth nodded.

He kissed her with all the emotion churning inside him. He told her how much he loved her over and over until they were both gasping for breath.

He pressed his forehead to hers. "I'm definitely okay with that, Doc," he finally murmured.

Elizabeth pulled away from him. "You'd better get out of here."

Confusion claimed that handsome face. "You're kidding about that part, right?"

She wagged her head side to side. "I have patients to see. The sooner I get through my schedule, the sooner I'll be home."

He grinned. "And we can have makeup sex."

Now there was that naughty side peeking out. "But we didn't have a fight," she countered.

"We did have a trial separation," he suggested.

He had her there.

"Go." She motioned toward the door. "We'll have all the makeup sex you want. Tonight."

He backed toward the door. She couldn't help watching the way he moved. So sexy. So chock-full of male confidence.

"I'll be waiting at your place. I'll even have dinner waiting."

Before she could question that promise he turned around and strolled out the door.

Her gaze narrowed. He said he'd have it ready, he didn't say he'd cook it.

Elizabeth pressed her hand to her tummy and smiled at the feeling of complete happiness that rushed through her.

Now she could rightfully say that she really did have it all.

And Joe Hennessey had definitely been worth the wait.

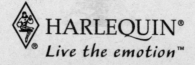

e◆HARLEQUIN.com

The Ultimate Destination for Women's Fiction

The eHarlequin.com online community is *the* place to share opinions, thoughts and feelings!

- Joining the community is easy, fun and **FREE!**

- Connect with **other romance fans** on our message boards.

- Meet your **favorite authors** without leaving home!

- **Share opinions** on books, movies, celebrities…and *more!*

Here's what our members say:

"I love the friendly and helpful atmosphere filled with support and humor."
—Texanna (eHarlequin.com member)

"Is this the place for me, or what? There is nothing I love more than 'talking' books, especially with fellow readers who are reading the same ones I am."
—Jo Ann (eHarlequin.com member)

Join today by visiting
www.eHarlequin.com!

If you enjoyed what you just read,
then we've got an offer you can't resist!

Take 2 bestselling love stories FREE!

Plus get a FREE surprise gift!

**#897 CRIME SCENE AT CARDWELL RANCH
by B.J. Daniels**
Montana Mystique
Former lovers reunite to dig up their families' torrid pasts and reveal the secret behind the skeleton found in an old dry well.

#898 SEARCH AND SEIZURE by Julie Miller
The Precinct
Kansas City D.A. Dwight Powers is a street-savvy soldier in a suit and tie. His latest case: saving the life of a woman caught up in an illegal adoption ring.

#899 LULLABIES AND LIES by Mallory Kane
Ultimate Agents
Agent Griffin Stone is a man that doesn't believe in happily ever after. Will private eye Sunny Loveless be able to change his mind?

#900 STONEVIEW ESTATE by Leona Karr
Eclipse
A young detective investigates the murderous history of a hundred-year-old mansion and unearths love amidst its treacherous and deceitful guests.

#901 TARGETED by Lori L. Harris
The Blade Brothers of Cougar County
Profiler Alec Blade must delve into the secrets of his past if he is to save the woman of his future.

#902 ROGUE SOLDIER by Dana Marton
When Mike McNair's former flame is kidnapped, he goes AWOL to brave bears, wolves and gunrunners in the Alaskan arctic cold.